A CANDLELIGHT

"Don't walk away fro...
harshly. . . .

"You won't escape m... whispered. "I'll pull your spirit back from whatever far distance you seek to send it."

He began to caress her lightly. "I may hurt you a bit this first time, Andrea," he murmured softly, "but I'll pleasure you too, as you will pleasure me."

They made love again the next morning with a passionate savagery Andrea would have thought herself incapable of. Last night had been farewell. This was for memory.

Dear Reader:

In response to your enthusiasm for Candlelight Ecstasy Romances, we are now increasing the number of titles per month from two to three.

We are pleased to offer you sensuous novels set in America, depicting modern American women and men as they confront the provocative problems of a modern relationship.

Throughout the history of the Candlelight line, Dell has tried to maintain a high standard of excellence, to give you the finest in reading pleasure. It is now and will remain our most ardent ambition.

Vivian Stephens
Editor
Candlelight Romances

THE
FACE OF
LOVE

Anne N. Reisser

A CANDLELIGHT ECSTASY ROMANCE

Published by
Dell Publishing Co., Inc.
1 Dag Hammarskjöld Plaza
New York, New York 10017

Dell ® TM 681510, Dell Publishing Co., Inc.

Candlelight Ecstasy Romance ™ is a trademark of
Dell Publishing Co., Inc., New York, New York.

ISBN: 0-440-12496-4

Printed in the United States of America

First printing—August 1981

CHAPTER ONE

If she kept her eyes fixed only on Johnny's face, she was almost able to pretend the head table didn't exist, to ignore the voluptuous redhead, who so determinedly pressed her cushiony breasts into the obliging arm of her table companion. Johnny looked at the frozen blankness of her face and realized the depth of the mistake he had made when he persuaded her to come to the party with him. He hadn't realized that it would affect her so badly.

"Would you prefer to go home now, Andy?" he asked softly. "There's no need to sit here and be tortured. I'm sorry, my dear. I didn't know it would be like this. I wouldn't have made you come with me if I'd realized . . ." His voice trailed off helplessly.

The blank eyes came up to focus on his, their normal soft gray shining with a steely glitter. "It's always like this." There was a shocking wealth of bitterness and hopeless pain in the husky voice. "She's not the first, and she's nowhere near the last. Others pay for the pain he causes, and I curse the ties that bind me to him. Husband, father . . . lecher! How can a woman know him for what he is and love him still? You tell me, Johnny. What qualities has such a man that he can command such devotion from a woman, any woman?"

7

Two fat tears sparkled in the inner corners of her eyes, and he pressed comforting hands over her small clenched fists, which pounded softly on the table between them in rhythmic agony as she talked. Fortunately the others at their table were already dancing, so they had relative privacy, but he knew that sooner or later someone would notice. He had to get her out and away before her control snapped absolutely.

"Andrea!" He spoke sharply, hoping to break through the low-voiced monotone. "Andy, stop it! I'll take you home. Pick up your purse, dear. We'll go home."

He made a move to rise, but she restrained him, laying a pinioning hand on his arm while she made a massive, visible effort to control herself. She fought and won her battle and then smiled shakily at him.

"I'm sorry, Johnny." Her smile was penitent and sincere. "I usually handle it better than this, but I stopped by the nursing home before we came here and the contrast was bitter. She is so frail and in so much pain and so damned *brave* about it all, and she loves the bas—" Johnny's fingers smothered the expletive gently but firmly.

"He's your father, Andy," he reminded her sternly.

"That doesn't change what he is, Johnny," she retorted hotly. "My mother lies dying by inches in a nursing home, twisted in agony, and my *father*"—the bitter scorn she packed into that word appalled him—"my father sits cosily beside his latest mistress, unsubtly disguised as his secretary, laughing and enjoying himself. And make no mistake, it's no pose hiding a tortured heart. He really is enjoying himself.

8

He visits Mother once or twice a week, professes love, and returns to the hot arms of his latest whore."

She looked at Johnny's white face and a caricature of a smile twisted her mouth. "Pretty, isn't it? And believe me, Johnny, dear friend that you are, you couldn't begin to guess the half of it. Maybe someday, after my mother dies, if you get me drunk and maudlin, I'll tell you the sordid whole."

This time her smile was dreamy, as if the dream were a nightmare. "The whole is beyond your wildest imaginings, my innocent friend. The unexpurgated saga of Devlin Thomas, stalwart husband and father. Oh, hell, dance with me, Johnny! The storm has blown itself out. I'll be a good girl now, and I won't even spit in his eye if we happen to come face to face with him on the dance floor."

Her smile now was tight but natural, and he stood, pulling her chair back to free her from the constricted space. She came to his arms gracefully, with that lithe economy of motion that characterized all her movements. If she were not a painter, she would have been a dancer, and the controlled elegance of her shapely body drew many an appreciative masculine eye.

It drew the eyes of two men at the head table, speculative gray and Viking blue. Gray-sprinkled black head and dark blond swiveled to trace the course of the dancing couple and the ignored redhead seated between them seethed, silently at first, but when pique overcame caution, audibly.

"Devlin," the voice grated shrilly and inappositely from such a pouted mouth. "Devlin, I want to dance now." She tugged at the arm she leaned against to command his attention. When his eyes came reluctantly to hers, she fluttered mascaraed lashes invitingly.

"We've only danced once tonight, Devlin," she reminded him and leaned forward slightly, allowing her décolletage to gape explicitly. Since she wore no bra, it was more explicit than might have been expected, and the man who raked her with jaded gray eyes was not yet proof against that invitation.

"Of course, Marta, my dear. Excuse us please, Breck," he said courteously to their companion.

"Certainly," came the smooth reply. "But before you go, do you know the man dancing with the black-haired woman in the blue dress? Does he work for the company or does she?"

"I know them both," was the curiously curt reply. "Shall I bring them to the table for an introduction?"

"Yes."

Royal command could not have been more sure of obedience, and blue eyes dismissed the standing couple to return to the swirling couples on the dance floor. It took a moment to locate the blue dress again, but once found, the blue eyes tenaciously kept the flash of color in view until, and after, the music blared its last drum-heavy note.

The eyes noted the approach of the older couple, redhead clinging limpetlike to the suited arm of her escort; saw the stiffening of the supple blue figure and the instinctive, abortive motion away from the speaking man; saw, narrow-eyed, the supportive, protective arm of the brown-haired escort go around the waist of the blue-dressed figure as the group of four turned to approach the head table.

The gold-haired giant rose as the two couples neared, and Andrea's stormy gray eyes traveled up the looming monolith to meet bright blue eyes under

10

hooded lids. Had it not been for Johnny, she would have had no compunction about refusing her father's request—huh, command described it better—to meet the new, or rather soon-to-be, owner of the company. As an executive vice-president, standing in for a stroke-felled president, her father played the part of host tonight. Johnny, lowly on the rungs of power, was vulnerable to any overt insult she might vent upon her revered parent.

Besides, Andrea had given her promise not to spit in his eye, overwhelming though the temptation might be. The memory of her mother's twisted, pain-tense body, which even merciful drugs could not make flaccid, churned bitter gall in the back of her throat, envenoming any words she could choke past that sharp-edged lump in her throat.

She barely listened to the smoothly practiced charm of her father's voice as he embarked on the introductions, but she did not miss the almost imperceptible start of surprise on the part of the giant when her father, oozing saccharine pride, announced their relationship.

"Ah, Breck, allow me to present my lovely daughter, Andrea, and her escort for the evening, one of our very bright young men, John McKay. Andrea, John, this is Breck Carson, soon to be your boss and mine, John."

Andrea was alerted to some undefined, strained inflection in her father's voice . . . she knew every lying intonation so well . . . but before she could analyze it, her automatically outstretched hand was taken in an engulfing clasp and her attention was captured by the voice that matched its hard strength so well.

"Miss Thomas," he acknowledged. "How remiss

of your father not to assure you and your escort a place at the head table."

He did not miss the steely flash in her level gray eyes and the sardonic curl of her full lips, nor the underlying chill in her husky contralto as she answered him politely but firmly.

"My father knows I prefer not to be on view at the head table, Mr. Carson, and I am sure he is surprised to see me here tonight. I do not usually appear at these functions and have done so tonight only at Johnny's behest."

She withdrew her hand from his clasp and tucked it back through Johnny's arm. "I have no connection with the company and am here only as Johnny's guest. I am not my father's hostess. Many others fill that role willingly."

Her voice was now a soft drawl and her gaze flickered dismissively over the redhead, who glared venomously at her. Andrea met her glare levelly, and Breck was interested to note that the redhead's green eyes fell before the contemptuous gray ones. He was even more interested to observe the dark flush that stained the face of her father, the father she so pointedly ignored with half-turned shoulder and averted face.

Was the girl condemnatory because of the obvious relationship between the father and his secretary? A daughter's jealousy over a diversion of attention away from herself, or deeper moral scruples? With a face and figure like hers, she certainly would not lack masculine attention herself, and latent fire burned beneath that icy glaze that so effectively cooled what he surmised would normally be dove-soft gray eyes. He came to a decision.

12

"McKay, I hope you'll allow me the pleasure of a dance with your charming date?"

It was phrased as a request, but rock-hard command underlay the smooth words. Even so, Johnny looked down questioningly at Andrea, and only after her tiny nod of acquiescence did he answer graciously, "Of course, Mr. Carson."

He relinquished Andrea's hand once more into Breck's keeping and smiled down at her. "I'll wait for you at our table, my dear. A pleasure to meet you, Mr. Carson." His smile to Breck was genuine, but his nod and "Mr. Thomas, Miss Stringer . . ." was perfunctory and just within the bounds of politeness.

Still never looking at her father, Andrea moved with economical grace to stand beside Breck, tilting her head back to meet his bright blue eyes. Her face was a perfect social mask, and he felt a violent impulse to force her response to him as a man. He already knew what he wanted from this woman, would have from this woman. Only the timing was at issue. Perhaps his own social mask was not impervious to her, because she went suddenly rigid and pulled her hand free of his.

"I believe you wished to dance, Mr. Carson?" she questioned him, lambent sparks flickering deep behind those gray eyes, which had suddenly gone depthless and impenetrable.

Andrea had read nothing in Breck's face. She had simply been overcome with a desire to go home, put her head down on her pillow, and cry. The accumulated stresses of the daily visits to her mother were wearing her down, and the confrontation with her father and his latest woman was nearly the final straw in a long and painful series of burdening straws. She saw Breck merely as a duty dance, to be

13

endured and, when done with, forgotte... She had not yet registered him as a man, a personality, only as piercing blue eyes and looming height. Her artist's eye would have enabled her to sketch him from swift memory, but only as the shell of a face, the personality behind it as yet undiscovered.

He led her onto the floor, and she automatically came into his arms. Her body was graceful and quick to follow his lead, but for all the sensual awareness she had of him, he might as well have been his own grandfather. Breck knew it and the realization stung.

He was determined to make her aware of him, to shock her awake if necessary. Was she in love with her escort? The thought was disturbingly unpalatable. What was the source of the all too obvious tension between father and daughter?

Breck was used to thinking on several levels at once, and while one portion of his mind considered the girl in his arms, another pondered the implications of the situation as it might affect one of the key executives of the company he was about to acquire. He needed more information. He had to untangle the twisted skeins of human relationships and lie them straight for his understanding.

Vigorous and ambitious, Breck Carson had come from nowhere with nothing. He used his body to win a sports scholarship and his brain to make the best use of the facilities the university offered. He had worked nights and studied days, and only an abundant vitality and the legacy of a splendidly healthy body kept him from burning himself to a cinder from the pace he maintained. He went after what he wanted and, thus far, whether it were a company or a woman, had gotten it.

Arrogant, ruthless, merciless . . . his enemies used

them all. Honest, brilliant, able . . . his friends and admirers retorted. None said gentle or benign.

They had danced in silence, bodies smoothly fitted together in the harmony of the music. Given the extra inches by her shoes, Andrea's head came just below the level of Breck's chin, and the faint fragrance of her hair had tantalized him ever since she had come obediently to his clasp. He could feel the silky softness of the blue-black shining cap of waves and curls . . . soft, not coarse. There was *nothing* coarse about the fine-boned elegance of this girl. Something sad and angry and hurt perhaps, but never gross or coarse.

"You said you had no connection with the company," he began probingly. "Are you still at school, then? Or do you occupy your days with Junior League and good works?"

"I visit the sick," she retorted with savage bitterness, betrayed by the memory of the afternoon she had spent, helpless and agonized, beside her mother's bed, parrying questions about the whereabouts of her father.

"I'm sorry!" she apologized immediately. "That was inexcusable." She continued in a forcedly normal tone. "Actually, I'm a commercial artist. I freelance, do book covers and illustrations, and when I have the time and energy, manage to dabble in oils and portraiture for the good of my artistic soul." She smiled whimsically up at him. "Art for art's sake may be good for the soul, but it tends to rubberize the checks you write for groceries and rent. Hence the descent into the mundane commercial world."

He probed further and hit a nerve.

"Are your oils good?"

"Yes," she admitted with simple candor.

15

"Well, surely your father could subsidize you until you—" He broke off abruptly as she lifted icy pale eyes to scan his face. No woman had ever looked at him with such chill contempt.

"I left my father's house when I was eighteen. I took nothing he had given me when I left and I take nothing from him now. I cannot help the blood that flows in my veins, and someday I shall change the name I bear. I am as polite as I am able when I am forced to endure his company, which is as infrequently as I can make it. The rest of the time I assiduously avoid seeing or thinking about him. Is there anything else you wish to know about the relationship between my father and myself?" She gave him no chance to answer, continuing in level, precise tones. "No? Good. The dance is ending. Please escort me to my table."

She slipped out of his arms as the music ended and turned toward the table where Johnny waited. Breck grasped her elbow firmly, intending to detain her, and swung her back to face him.

"Don't walk away from me, Andrea," he ordered harshly.

She looked down at the hand that was clamped above her elbow and then back up to meet his blue eyes squarely. "Then walk beside me. I do not care to dance again, and I wish to return to my date. I'm very tired, and he'll take me home. It was a mistake for me to come. I knew better . . . I won't make this mistake ever again."

"I'll take you home."

They started threading their way slowly through the dancers who remained on the floor. Andrea was at the end of her tether, and she knew if she didn't go home soon, she'd lose what thin shreds of control

16

still remained within her. Breck Carson, with his probing and prodding, had lifted the thin scabs of her wounds, and the poison that festered beneath was oozing irresistibly forth. The reserve she had so painfully cultivated these past three years seemed easily shattered by this dynamic, imperious man. Instead of ignoring his questions, she flew at him in rage, exposing her vulnerability with hasty, anguished words.

She was so tired. She had been working against a deadline for the past week, and the late nights and tension had taken a heavy toll. The visits to her mother every afternoon battered her emotionally and also forced her to work long, late hours to make up the time lost at the nursing home.

Then, this morning, she had mailed off the completed work, accepting the registered mail receipt from the mail clerk with a dazzling smile and a gay quip. As she reentered her apartment her phone had begun to ring. Johnny caught her in a mood to celebrate. He offered dinner and dancing, and not until they were in the car had he disclosed that the price she would pay for her evening out was to attend a company party given in honor of the new owner.

She had remonstrated, but the lateness of the hour and Johnny's imperative need to make an appearance for form's sake overrode her well-founded objections. It wasn't really Johnny's fault, Andrea admitted fairly to herself. He knew of the estrangement, but not of its depth and breadth. He was new to the company, though an old friend from her high school days, and had been away at college at the time she moved out and her mother entered the nursing home.

Rumor had informed Johnny of the liaison between Devlin Thomas and his lush secretary, but he had not expected the blatancy of their association and the subsequent effect it was to have on Andy's nerves. Now he wished with all his heart that he had resisted temptation and been content to take Andy out for dinner another night. But she'd been so busy lately. . . .

He watched glumly as Andrea swirled and circled in the arms of his new boss. That was another thing. He didn't like the way Breck looked at her. He was attracted, but then most men were. When she was happy, Andy sparkled. Even strained and subdued she was a beautiful challenge, with a remote reserve appealing to both the predatory and protective instincts. Breck Carson was a man who took what he wanted, and Johnny hoped he didn't decide that he wanted Andy.

Breck's assured statement that he would take Andrea home would have in no way reassured the anxious Johnny. Andrea did not slow her steady exit from the dance floor, but she did answer back over her shoulder.

"You're the guest of honor," she reminded him, determined to be polite.

"I'm also the boss," was his retort. "If I want to leave, who's going to tell me to stay?"

"I will," Andrea flared again, "if you're only planning to leave because you want to take me home. I came with Johnny, and I'll leave with Johnny."

He tested her. "I'm Johnny's boss too."

At that she whirled, eyes no longer icily chill. Burning anger blazed in eyes gone dark with fury, and a hot flush flagged her high cheekbones. "Let's get something straight, Mr. Carson. First, you're not *my* boss and second, I don't blackmail." She looked closely at his impassive face, surprised to see no signs

18

of anger. She continued with less heat. "And third, you wouldn't use your position as owner of this company to try to take another man's girl away. It's not your style."

"Are you his girl?"

"I'm his date. I'm no man's girl."

He gave a satisfied nod. "Good. I'll return you to your date. Just remember, when you're my date, I'll expect the same standard of loyalty."

If he had hoped to achieve a reaction to this pronouncement, he was disappointed. Andrea was exhausted and had the beginnings of a throbbing headache behind her right eye. The smoke and noise and blaring music completed the job the evening's events began, and now her dearest wish was to go home and sleep.

She forged steadily through the obstructing couples until she came to the table where Johnny stood waiting. With a polite half smile she mouthed the conventional phrases to Breck and then laid a beseeching hand on Johnny's arm.

"Johnny, dear, I'd like to go home now. May we leave, please?"

Johnny looked tenderly down at the weary, shadow-smudged face and agreed instantly. Both men watched as she gathered her purse from the table, and Johnny sprang forward with eager hands to help her into her lightweight jacket, which he lifted from the back of her chair. She thanked him with a small smile and tucked her hand into the crook of his bent elbow.

Breck watched them leave, not returning to the head table until they had actually left the room. He ignored all the speculative looks cast his way. Whatever he did would be food for gossip, and rumor

19

would swiftly make the most of his singling out Andrea. He had danced with no woman the whole evening, not even the all too willing Marta, nor had he planned to dance until he had seen Andrea across the room.

Social conventions had never overly concerned him. He used them when they had value to him and ignored them the rest of the time. He feared no man's censure nor cared for anyone's good opinion of him save his own. His business reputation was impeccable. He was acknowledged to be ruthless, shrewd, and possessed of an almost uncanny ability to acquire and reanimate faltering companies. Some he kept and some he sold, once they were healthy again, at no small profit for himself. Only two men had ever tried to cheat him. He broke them both. His own word was his bond, but he was known to keep some of the finest available legal minds on yearly retainer.

Of his personal life little was known except that there was one. No man with such a physical presence and cynically knowing eyes could be supposed not to have one, but even his most assiduous detractors could find no leverage in his personal life. He had escorted many attractive women, but was linked with none. Gossip columnists found him poor fare and, moreover, dangerous fare, as one unwary columnist discovered after an unsuccessfully defended suit for slander beggared him and disastrously affected the balance sheet of a newspaper that had once employed him. If Breck's name appeared in the columns now, it was as a mere passing reference. He was ferociously discreet and willing to go to some lengths to remain so.

The sooner she could forget the evening's events,

the better. Andrea laid her head wearily back against the head rest of the seat in Johnny's car. She acknowledged that she needed a holiday, but knew she couldn't take one. Her mother depended heavily on her daily visits, and after her discussion with the doctor today, she accepted the fact that all too soon she would be free to go where she would and do as she pleased. There would be nothing more to hold her to this place.

Three years of faithful daily visits, of searching the stores for amusing and distracting presents. It was fortunate that she had been successful as a commercial artist. Out of season fruit to tempt a laggard appetite and out of season flowers to interest and brighten four monotonous walls don't come cheaply. She never went to see her mother without some small offering . . . a new book, a puzzle or new music cassette, or perhaps a wickedly drawn cartoon to illustrate an amusing story she would relate to her mother. Love and pity made her endlessly inventive, and the room that was her mother's prison had the character of a home, insofar as such a room can.

Andrea had prevailed upon the proprietors of the nursing home to allow her to replace the usual curtains and bed cover with ones she herself supplied. Those she changed often to give her mother a variation in surroundings. Textures, colors, hand painted fabrics . . . she utilized them all to broaden the constricted environment her mother was condemned to endure.

The nurses admired and adopted her ideas where they could so other long-term patients benefited from Andrea's determined refusal to allow shackling pain to narrow her mother's life to days of dreary sameness. When she changed the curtains and bedspread, she passed the discarded ones on to some other long-resident sufferer. Books and bibelots made the rounds of rooms, and her lightning fast cartoons and caricatures could generally draw a smile from the dourest of patients.

The price Andrea paid was not in hard-earned money alone. She paid in time, in late nights racing to meet deadlines. She paid in smiles and cheerful words while her heart was dripping bloody tears. Her eyes were sad and wise before their time . . . to watch the anguish of a loved one is often harder than to experience the physical torment oneself.

And now . . . her long vigil was drawing inexorably to a close. The doctor had been blunt this afternoon. The dosages of merciful opiate had been increased again. It was the beginning of that long, final slide to surcease from all pain, forerunner to the time of release from the days of purgatory for her mother . . . and not only the purgatory of physical pain.

As much as she could Andrea had avoided an overlap of visiting time with her father. Her mother knew her feelings toward her father. When and while he made his duty visits, Andrea left. She was polite, as to a stranger newly met. More she could not be, even for her mother's ease. Infinite forgiveness was beyond her. Her mother was a saint, purified by love and pain. Andrea was human and she hated.

"I am sorry, Andy." Johnny apologized again, breaking into her train of thought.

"It's okay, Johnny," she assured him. "You couldn't have known. It's not something one talks about . . . the fact that one despises one's father."

The light from the streetlamps that flickered past aged and harshened the contours of her bone structure. In the glances he could spare from concentration on the road, Johnny didn't miss the grim set of her mouth or the controlled tenseness in the clear line of her jaw.

She was much changed. Even in high school she had been oddly mature, never giggly or gawky. There had been an innate air of reserve to set her apart from the common run of girls, but in spite of, or perhaps because of, this same reserve, she was one of the most popular people in her class. Cheerleader, homecoming princess, student council officer . . . all had been hers without her seeking them.

But now? No flashes of impish humor brightened the grave, level gaze. Control, not serenity, sculpted the planes of her face. Johnny longed to probe, but there was a daunting impenetrability about her that even an old friend hesitated to confront. Even with his extra years he felt a youth yet to her maturity.

Andrea hoped that he would be content to take her home and leave her there. By clock hours it was still early, but her day had been years long. When he parked in front of the building that housed her apartment, she made the small but unmistakable preparations for imminent departure that told him he wouldn't be wise to attempt to detain her.

Sensitive to nuances and withal no fool, he promptly got out of the car and walked around to help her out. They shared the noisy elevator to the top floor in silence and traversed the short hall to her door. She had her key ready, and it slid smoothly into the lock.

"May I call you in a few days, Andy?" His question was diffident.

"Of course, Johnny, dear. Please do." She tried to inject as much warmth as possible into the permission, but exhaustion made it ring flat. Just now she didn't care whether she ever saw him again or not. Any emotion, even that of friendship, seemed to require too great an effort.

Obediently Johnny kept his good-night kiss brief and as nearly passionless as he could manage, and after bidding her not to watch him to the elevator, he left her. Andrea took him at his word and went directly into her apartment and locked the door behind her.

As the dead bolt snicked home she sagged back against the door, head bowed, shoulders drooping. She stayed that way for a long moment and then, with a thrust of her shoulders, levered herself away from the door. Her footsteps clicked a dispirited rhythm across the polished wooden floor, muffled momentarily when she cut across the corner of the area rug near the couch, heading toward the rectangle of light that spilled toward her from the bedroom door.

As she entered her bedroom she tossed her purse on the single bed and went directly to the wall-to-wall, ceiling-to-floor, flower graphic decorated curtain, which matched the bedspread and the curtains at the window. When she had supervised the partitioning of the expansive open space of this building's top floor into rooms, there were no closets. With typical ingenuity she hung poles on chains attached to eye bolts driven into the ceiling beams and masked the contrivance with the false wall of the curtain. The fabric was hand printed with her own designs, as were the matching spread and curtains. She had painted the fabric herself, and a very talented friend transformed the lengths of cloth into a quilted spread and drapes.

For the first year after she had left her father's

house Andrea had lived frugally in a small, very cramped furnished apartment. Then, as she began to find a larger measure of financial ease—she was really very talented—she started to look for something more spacious. By chance she heard of a building, once derelict offices, that some enterprising young people were renovating and turning into apartments.

She had investigated and found the terms agreeable and the top floor space ideal. It had large windows and a good exposure in the area she decided to make her studio, and when the owners promised to install a bathroom, kitchen, and room partitions at her direction, she signed the lease without a qualm.

She had never regretted it. She had privacy and space and if not much furniture, each piece she had was good, lovingly chosen after much searching. The partitions between the rooms were thin, but with only herself to consider . . . there was only one apartment per floor . . . the lack of soundproofing was no drawback. Color made the apartment cheery where lack of furniture might have chilled and emptied it. And it was hers alone, her citadel from which she issued forth, her refuge where she retreated to gather strength for the next day.

Andrea hung up her jacket and dress, lined her shoes neatly on the floor, and headed naked toward the bathroom to wash her face free of the light make-up she wore and to brush her teeth. She tossed her underclothes into the wicker basket that was her clothes hamper, creamed and cleansed her face, and grimaced unconsciously at the minty bite of the toothpaste she was currently using.

Just before she slid between the smooth sheets, she shoved a cassette into her portable tape recorder,

25

which lay on the floor beside the head of her bed. She had no formal religious alliances, but at times found the sonorous rhythms of stately Gregorian chants calming and soothing. As the blended male voices began to drone softly into the stillness of the room, she burrowed into the sheets and waited for her body warmth to drive away the chill from her nest of covers. By the time the tape had wound its way to the end and shut off automatically, she was deeply asleep, curled tightly in a defensive ball, which relaxed only slightly as the night progressed toward the dawn.

She lay abed the next morning past a leisurely eight o'clock. When she raced a deadline, she generally rose at first light to begin work, but all her current commissions, except the one she had just completed, had no time limits save that of her need for the money they would bring. Her bank account was comfortably red-blooded, preserved from anemia by the infusion of checks for three recently completed assignments and the soon to be due check for the material she had sent off yesterday.

She showered, shampooed, and blew dry her glossy black cap of curls and dressed for the day. Since today was not to be a working day, she chose a simple cotton knit top, teamed with a gaily patterned skirt. She always wore vivid colors when she went on her visits to her mother, and today would be no exception. It was fortunate that she had the coloring to carry off the dramatic colors.

When she investigated the contents of her refrigerator, she realized what her morning's activities would have to be. She cubed some leftover steak and added it to the last two eggs, which were scrambling in the skillet. There was no bread, not even a stale heel, and she remembered she had used both heels at noon the day before yesterday for a hasty peanut butter and jelly sandwich.

She checked the freezer and the cupboard she laughingly dubbed the pantry. Not too bad . . . not a complete restock, then. She just needed the perishables and a nibbler's supply of fruit, oh, and another jar of peanut butter. Never run out of peanut butter, she admonished herself silently. It's stood between you and starvation many a time during a rushed assignment.

Just before she left on her shopping expedition, she called the nursing home to bid her mother good morning and ask, as always, if there was anything special she could get before she came for her afternoon visit. And sadly, as always, the reply was, "Nothing, dear."

No, there was indeed nothing. What her mother needed most of all, a faithful husband and legs that walked, was beyond Andrea's power to give her.

Determined not to be enmeshed in a black mood, she made a hasty exit from the apartment. As she headed for the fire stairs she heard the muted burr of the phone and debated for a moment whether to return and answer it. It would not be her mother, but it might possibly be her father, calling to take her to task for her behavior last night. Perhaps he wished to protect his image before his new boss.

That thought made her decide. She entered the stairwell, and as the fire door closed behind her the phone sounds were cut in mid-ring. She usually walked down the stairs and quite frequently up them as well unless burdened by packages. Her life was far more sedentary than she would have liked, and it was a small way of exercising.

27

Just before lunch time she returned, riding up in the elevator in deference to the two heavy bags of groceries she was balancing precariously in her arms. She knew she should have brought them up one at a time, but was loath to make two trips when one would do. It took some rather involved contortions, balancing one bag on an uplifted knee, steadied by her arm, to allow her to reach the sixth floor button, but the elevator began to rise with the bags still safely intact.

She negotiated the short hall to her front door rather quickly, because she could feel an ominous tear beginning at the side of the bag where a damp patch had weakened the paper. It was her preoccupation with the sacks she carried that caused her to miss seeing the flowers immediately.

They were certainly lovely enough to command attention, and the vibrant crimson of the topmost buds soon caught the corner of her eye. She knelt before her door and eased the grocery bags gingerly to the floor. From that position she was nearly nose to nose with a glorious arrangement of roses, all half-opened buds, shading in color from a pure virgin white to pale then deeper pink, and on through a spectrum ending in a clear, passion-dark crimson.

It should have been ostentatious, but instead it was breathtaking. A chaste cream envelope was tucked amid the glossy green foliage, but she left it where it was for the moment. The groceries were her first priority, and if she didn't get that one bag inside, she'd be chasing oranges down the hall.

After attending to the groceries, she carefully carried the vase of flowers inside, setting it on the dining table. Some water had slopped over, so she mopped it up and slid a protective plate beneath the vase lest it leave a ring on the table. Only then did she take out the envelope and open it to withdraw the card.

An aggressive black scrawl slashed across the flat card and she deciphered the message curiously: "I'll pick you up for dinner at seven p.m. Friday night. Wear a long dress."

It was signed with the initials B.C. Who the devil was B.C., and what the hell did he mean by sending her such an outrageous message? She had met a new doctor at the nursing home, and she could tell he'd like to ask her out. His name was Robert Culhane, but he was rather shy and this—she snapped the card with an irritated fingernail—didn't seem at all his style.

Her forehead creased in perplexed thought, and she tapped the edge of the card meditatively against her front teeth. Was it perhaps Johnny's idea of an amende honorable for the debacle of last night? She dismissed that idea almost before it had a chance to form. Johnny would have to forgo all his lunches for a month to come up with the wherewithal for such an expensive invitation to dinner. And . . . not his style either. If he gave her flowers, they would probably be filched from his mother's garden and all she ever managed to grow were zinnias!

Style. That struck a chord somewhere. Someone aggressive and blunt, used to taking what he wanted. Two bright blue eyes floated into her inner vision. Good God! Breck Carson, the new boss man.

Her first thought was, What arrogant nerve! Her second, He can't be serious! and her third, as she looked at the decisive black writing again and from the card to the flowers, He is serious. Do I want to go?

She hesitated, then walked over to the telephone.

29

She flipped through the phone book, ran a slim forefinger down a line of listings, and then dialed. When the switchboard answered, she said crisply, "Connect me with Mr. Carson's office, please."

She waited, drumming suddenly agitated fingers on the table while the receiver spat forth a series of clicks and buzzes, and when another female voice informed her that she now spoke to Mr. Carson's secretary, Andrea drew in a deep breath and said, "This is Andrea Thomas. I wish to speak with Mr. Carson, please."

The impersonal businesslike tones underwent a dramatic change. "Oh, Miss Thomas. I'm Miss Jenkins. Mr. Carson told me to expect your call. He told me to assure you that he would indeed be back by Friday." The secretary assumed a chatty, confiding tone and continued, "He called me from the airport just before his plane took off, and gave me my instructions. I've just received confirmation, in fact, that tickets for the opening night will be waiting at the box office for you and Mr. Carson." Her voice held distinct tones of awe. "The tickets are coming directly from Devon Harmon, you know. Isn't he just super? Mr. Carson is a personal friend of his, and to think that he'll be at the opening night party afterward . . ." Her voice trailed off in near ecstasy.

Andrea fought the impulse to break into hysterical giggles. The voice chattered relentlessly onward. "Was there anything else, Miss Thomas? Mr. Carson gave me strict instructions that if there was anything you needed, I was to put myself at your disposal." Her voice fairly quivered with eagerness to please.

"No. Thank you, Miss Jenkins," Andrea responded dryly. "I believe that just about covers everything.

You're sure Mr. Carson won't be back before Friday?"

This unleashed another spate of words. "Oh, no, Miss Thomas. In fact, he had been scheduled to be gone the full two weeks, but I was able to clear his reservation to return late Sunday night without too much trouble, and he said he would take care of coming in on Friday himself."

There was nothing left to say. Andrea extricated herself from the conversation before Miss Jenkins swept them both away on another floodtide of eloquence. She rather hoped the woman had good dictation and typing speeds as part of her qualifications because discretion did not seem to be one of her secretarial skills. Andrea had a feeling that Miss Jenkins would not long reign as Breck Carson's confidential secretary. Confiding she was. Confidential she was not!

Mechanically she began to put the groceries away, moving between the counter and the refrigerator as she pondered all that the voluble Miss Jenkins had disclosed. Somehow Breck had managed to arrange for tickets for the new, highly touted Devon Harmon play, and the opening night performance at that. The play had been sold out for the entire first month's run for the past six weeks and tickets for later performances were devilishly hard to get. Even the scalpers weren't able to find tickets for the early performances, but Breck had managed to do so between the time Andrea left him at the party and before his plane took off.

She shivered slightly. The man wielded power.

While she ate a small chef's salad Andrea tried to call Breck's features to mind. She could see only piercing blue eyes. She went into her studio and came

31

back out with a block of sketch paper and an artist's pencil. If her mind could not tell her, her fingers would. She began to slash swift, dramatic strokes on the paper, her salad forgotten.

When she was done, she ripped off the top sheet of paper and propped it against the vase of flowers. The crisp, aggressive lines of the portrait contrasted sharply with the sensuous softness of the flowers. A very disturbing man looked back at her.

It was a direct gaze, clear and uncompromising. If there was any softness in this man, it was buried too deeply for her fingers to find. He liked his own way and knew how to get it. Possessive . . . what I have, I hold . . . it was there in the thrust of the squared-off chin. The mouth was firm, controlled, but yet she knew, almost as though she had seen and felt it, the lips could soften into sensuality and spark wild hunger where they touched.

Handsome? No, too strong a face for that sleek descriptive. Some Viking ancestor had left his seed behind when he came a-raiding, to reincarnate in bone and blood in these modern times. An imperious nose to match an imaginary winged helm and springing dark gold hair, worn slightly long, but burnished with an almost metallic sheen.

Disturbing and . . . dangerous. A warrior who would take a captive or a concubine and leave her behind without a qualm when it was time for the next foray. Her hand went out to crush the sketch and then drew back slowly. What the hand had seen, the mind should remember. She would keep the sketch as a reminder.

CHAPTER TWO

Her mother was much the same, soft brown eyes faded and sunken, the color leeched away by constant pain. Her hair, once a thick, rich auburn, was gray and sparsely lank. Andrea had arranged for a hairdresser to come twice a week to condition and style it, but when the body's vitality is gone, no skill can keep the hair from reflecting the truth. Her skin was crumpled, not with the soft lines of graceful age but sharply grooved and scored, as though a stiff piece of paper had been twisted between two hands and only roughly flattened out again, leaving sharp corners and deep creases to mar its once smooth surface.

The wasted, twisted body was shielded from sight by a softly shirred nightgown and matching bed jacket, but the stick-thin arms with ropy blue veins and fleshless fingers told the tale. Her mother was forty-seven years old. Her hands belonged to a crone of double her years.

Andrea's heart wept but her face smiled as she bent to kiss her mother's withered cheek. She rummaged in her purse and pulled forth a brightly papered package, tied with a broad velvet ribbon which needed only a tug to release itself. Her mother loved the feel of soft-napped fabrics and could stroke the rich blue width as though it were an Angora-soft pet.

When the paper was laid back, a spring-flowered muslin sachet bag was revealed and the evocative scent of old lavender drifted up to tease the nostrils. Jeanne Thomas lifted the bag in tremulous hands, the better to inhale the memory-rich scent. Small pleasures alone were left her and scent enjoyment was one. Her old, accustomed perfumes turned acid sour on her skin now, but Andrea insured that her soaps and lotions had pleasing fragrances and that her bedwear hung in scented proximity to pomander balls until it lay soft and aromatic against her sere skin.

"We'll pin the bag to your pillow so that you need only turn your head to catch the scent easily," Andrea assured her and suited actions to words. The pin she used to anchor the bag in place was an enameled purple and gold pansy face, a charming little frippery which did the job as well as the utilitarian safety pin another might have used. A small touch, but small touches lifted the spirit, and when one's whole existence is bound within four sterile walls, small touches and small irritations assume magnified importance.

"Thank you, darling." Jeanne thanked her daughter for more than the sachet. "I'll enjoy it in the night."

Andrea's heart twisted. The wakeful dark nights when her mother twisted on the rack of pain and fought the silent losing battle. Even the ever stronger doses of mercy could not totally cage the sharp-clawed tiger which gnawed her spine.

"How is the painting you're working on now coming along?" Jeanne asked. When a painting was finished, Andrea always brought it to show to her mother and, if Jeanne desired, arranged to hang it for several days so that she might enjoy it before it went to those who commissioned it or had bought it. Her oils always sold well, but the commercial assignments took less time and paid much better for the time involved.

Time was subjective but not elastic, and since she never skimped on her visits to her mother, the time must come from that allotted to serious painting. Consequently there was a backlog of commissions that she worked on as she was able, or when the prodding from impatient clients was more importunate than usual.

"It's almost finished. I should be able to bring it for you to see sometime next week. I'm very pleased with it. Sylvia Carrington saw it in embryo and paid a deposit on the spot. She's been amazingly, for her, patient, especially since she plans to make it the focal point for her living room and is holding the decorator off until I've completed it. She only calls me once a week. When I was working on the one she has hanging in her guest room, she called me twice a week until I threatened to wipe the whole thing out with turpentine." Andrea grinned. "That scared her so badly that I didn't hear from her again until I called her to come pick it up. You remember that one, don't you? The field of wild flowers with the single bleached tree in the left foreground? You liked it so much, we left it hanging for a week and a half."

"Oh, yes. That was one of my favorites. You could almost see the flowers move as the wind passed by. You brought me a bouquet of the same kind of flowers that week. I remember it well. I held them in my hands and imagined I had just picked them from the field. I even felt the texture of that dried, dead tree . the smooth peeled places and the patches of rough bark. It was a very good painting, Andrea." Her voice was quiet and dreaming, perhaps back in time when she could have indeed walked in the field and touched the tree

Andrea half turned her head, looking out the window. Her voice was steady but her eyes were moist. "I'm glad it gave you pleasure, Mother. Would you like to see it again? I can borrow it from Sylvia for as long as you like."

"Yes, I think I would." Jeanne's voice still had that reminiscent tone.

"I'll bring it with me tomorrow, Mother," Andrea promised.

They talked of other things. Andrea read the newspaper to her mother and then several chapters of a current best seller. There was a rack to hold the book at a comfortable angle so that Jeanne need only turn the pages, but she loved the sound of her daughter's voice, husky and musical, so Andrea read aloud whenever and from whatever Jeanne requested.

Soft-footed and smiling, a nurse came in to give the early evening shot and pills, the signal for Andrea to prepare to leave. While the drugs held greatest potency her mother could sleep, recouping somewhat the strength pain drained away, but the credit and debit sides never balanced out. Always the slow, remorseless seepage. The cup never filled again to the same level, but ever lower. One day the ebb would turn no more.

Andrea bent to kiss the proffered cheek farewell as she did in greeting, but her mother's attention was fixed on the brief oblivion the nurse held in capable hands. Her good-bye was preoccupied, almost curt,

36

and Andrea smiled sadly at the waiting nurse, receiving knowing commiseration in return. They came, they went, but the pain stayed. To drive it back for even a short time was a boon she would not delay or deny her mother for an instant.

The days before Friday were busy. Several new assignments came in, the flowers on her dining table opened to full glory and then blown, began to drop their petals. Andrea obtained the loan of the picture she had promised her mother by agreeing to hurry completion of Sylvia's new picture. She shopped, she visited her mother, and sometimes in the solitude of her apartment she wondered how long she could keep the pace.

On Thursday she decided to treat herself to a dress worthy of a Devon Harmon opening night. The check for the commission she had mailed off the day she met Breck arrived in the morning's mail and with uncharacteristic extravagance she decided it would be symbolically meet to use most of it to outfit herself appropriately. The dress she chose did indeed consume a goodly portion of the check and was worth every paint-spattered penny.

It was black and anything but basic. She took it with her when she went to see her mother and even slipped it on to model it. Several of the nurses came in to "ooh" and "aah" and to comment enviously about her good fortune in getting to see Devon Harmon. When her mother proudly announced that Andrea was going to the opening night cast party as well, the exclamations redoubled in force. Andrea was adjured to remember Devon Harmon's every word and facial expression to enable her to render a faithful accounting the next day.

Friday came and, although the week could not be said to have dragged, she greeted the morning with almost a sigh of relief. She was, she admitted honestly, looking forward to the evening. Though she was not particularly overawed by the Devon Harmon mystique, he was a fine actor. The story line of the play was intriguing and, after all, a first night is a first night!

She put in a short morning at work, finishing Sylvia's picture. With proper precautions she could take it for her mother to see and enjoy over the weekend before delivering it to Sylvia early next week. A day to dry, and she'd hang it for her mother, unframed, tomorrow.

Precisely at seven that night an imperative knock rapped twice on the front door. Andrea opened the door and stepped back, inviting him in by a gesture with her left hand.

He really was magnificently male! Her fingers had not lied. The severe elegance of his evening attire fitted the massively broad shoulders and narrow waist without a wrinkle. No off-the-peg rental tux would fit him, and he wore the formal clothes with an accustomed ease speaking of casual familiarity.

He stepped into the apartment and she closed the door behind him. She turned back to face him and discovered he had not taken his eyes from her. His face was inscrutable, but his eyes were a bright, dark-pupiled blue. His intense gaze made her nervous.

"G-good evening, Breck." Not knowing what else to do, she held out a shy hand to him.

In a totally unexpected maneuver he used her outstretched hand to pull her gently near and dropped a petal-soft kiss directly on her surprised mouth, for

38

all the world as though they were old friends meeting again after an absence of months.

While she gaped speechlessly at him he said in satisfaction, "I knew I'd remembered."

"Remembered? Remembered what?" she asked faintly.

"How beautiful you are . . . and how much I was looking forward to kissing you. Although," he considered judiciously, "that really wasn't much of a kiss. Care to try again?"

She moved hastily backward. He grinned suddenly and remarked, "Pity. You've made it very difficult for me to concentrate on anything else this past week."

Before she could respond he turned to survey the room, and she was sure not an item escaped that incisive gaze. "Very nice. Your own work?" He had moved to stand before the focal point of the living room, a fantasy underseascape of swirling blues and greens interspersed with streaks of yellow, red, and orange, which coalesced into fantastic coral shapes as one looked. He peered closely at the upper right corner and she smiled quietly. He'd seen the mermaid's face, her own, which had the disconcerting habit of becoming visible, only to vanish in a clever optical illusion. The face was attatched to the faithful rendering of her own nicely curved upper body, which was in turn melded into a sinuous fish's tail.

It was really quite a modest work, because it was impossible to hold the focus of the eyes long enough to make out much specific detail. One blink and the mermaid coyly dissolved again into blue-green formless mist.

He chuckled. "She's quite a tease." He looked Andrea up and down as though considering just how faithful the rendering of the mermaid had been. "You were much too modest."

Andrea stiffened and her eyes sparked with incipient ire.

"You told me your oils were merely good," he continued smoothly, leaving her to wonder if he had indeed meant the double entendre. "You are extremely talented. Have you many completed canvases ready? Enough for a small show?"

"I'm afraid not," she said a trifle coolly, more than a little suspicious of his bland innocence. "Almost all of my canvases are commissioned and those that aren't sell too rapidly for me to build up enough material for a full-scale show. The only ones I have on hand are a few personal ones which are for my own pleasure and are not for sale. I do have one I've just completed, but it's been sold too. I'm to deliver it next week, but you may see it now if you'd like."

She took him into the studio and flicked on the overhead lights. She had used a variation of the technique which had achieved the mermaid's elusive qualities to impart a sense of breeze-directed movement to the peaceful woodland glade. No animal life was visible, but one felt that only seconds before, the open space had teemed with motion. The viewer, an intruder, had just sent the glade's inhabitants scurrying for cover and even now eyes peered, hidden in the dappled, shifting shadows, waiting for the alien presence to leave so that a normal routine could resume. The ear was tricked into listening for the rustle of leaves, depending on the message from the eyes that the leaves had just moved.

He moved to view the painting from several angles, shook his head, and stepped back to her side again. "Amazing. The textures of the bark and leaves, the shifting light and shade . . . add scent and sound and we're there." He looked sternly down at her. "You waste time on commercial art when you are capable of this?" He waved an expressive hand at the painting.

"This," she in turn waved toward the painting, "is not done in a day, nor yet a week. Some day, perhaps . . . but for now, I have to eat and I have other obligations." None of which are your business, her tone implied.

"And I think I'd better feed you." He smiled down at her. "You're obviously hungry."

And you're obviously a master of the innuendo, she thought rather sourly, implying my temper and perhaps my manners suffer when I'm hungry. Well, Mr. Carson, if I'm ungracious, you're nosy, and she firmly flicked the lights in the studio off as they left the room.

She gathered her wrap and purse and switched off all the lights except one small one by the couch. The diffuse illumination made a dark mystery of the sea scene, heightening the illusion of restless waters, and Breck shook his head in admiring bewilderment.

"I'll be damned if I see how you achieve that effect. If I touched the painting, I'd expect my fingers to come away wet."

She stood by the door, the key for the dead bolt in her hand. "There's a small one in my bedroom in which a school of fish appear and then disappear. That one took me two months, off and on. It was the first one that really achieved the effect I was after." Her face shadowed. "I was seventeen when I finished it."

She locked the door behind them and dropped the key into her purse. She headed automatically for the stairwell and then caught herself. "Sorry. I usually go up and down the stairs. It's my one regular form of exercise; but not"—she grinned—"when I'm all gussied up."

When they were in the car and driving toward wherever he was taking her to dinner—he hadn't said and she didn't ask—he returned to the subject of the painting she had just completed. He wanted to know to whom she had sold it and she told him, explaining that Sylvia also had another one of her paintings. She wondered why he had wanted to know, so she asked him.

"Because I want to buy it from her," he admitted bluntly.

"Oh," she responded, rather blankly. She supposed it was flattering that he liked her work so well, but she was reminded of the ruthless determination which had appeared so clearly in the sketch she'd done of him and she was uneasy. Her work was a part of her, a piece of her thoughts and skills, and she wasn't sure she wanted him to own any part of her, even a painting.

"I don't think you'll be able to convince Sylvia to sell," she advised him. "She's waited several months for this particular painting, and she's planning to redecorate her living room around it."

He merely smiled slightly and began to talk of other things. She followed his lead obediently and they talked amiably and volubly through an excellent dinner, right up until the curtain rose on the first act.

Andrea discovered that Breck had a dry, incisive wit, when he cared to display it, and a keen, exciting mind. They argued, agreed, and argued again on a broad range of subjects, and while she could not

42

match him for depth of knowledge in all areas, she knew she gave a good account of herself.

She didn't bore him and more than once his deep chuckle rumbled forth as she scored with some sally. Halfway through dinner she realized, with some amusement, that he had deftly put her at ease. Her initial wariness had melted away beneath the balm of his charm. She was truly enjoying herself, more so than she could ever remember, and it wasn't just the delicious dinner and the prospect of a first-rate play. It was the man himself.

When they left the restaurant, she made no demur when he tucked her hand beneath his arm, covering it possessively with his own large hand as they strolled to the theater, which was only a block away.

The timing was perfect. The tickets were waiting and they were escorted to their superb seats with unhurried leisure. There was time to settle comfortably and to scan the program and then, almost as if at their specific command, the house lights dimmed, the curtain rose, and the play began.

Andrea smiled. She laughed and then she cried. She pulled herself away from the world the actors had created with an effort when intermission came, and as if he understood and was giving her time to readjust to reality, Breck led her silently out into the foyer, tucked her securely behind some scruffy potted nameless plant, and left her. He seemed hardly gone a minute before he materialized again, confronting her with two brimming champagne glasses carried steadily in his hands. She accepted one readily and sipped, cocking an eyebrow at him in surprise at its quality.

His answering grin was oddly boyish. "Private stock," he explained with a chuckle. "Devon arranged to have a bottle left for me in the theater manager's office."

"Beats waiting in line," she murmured. A thought struck her. "Are you, what's the term, an angel?"

"Not for this play," he denied, "but I have backed a couple of his plays before. He hopes I will again in the future." A faint lacing of cynicism threaded his voice, and he sipped the champagne as though it had suddenly soured slightly.

"You might have missed out on a good investment," she said lightly and led the conversation into a discussion of the play so far. Her diversionary tactics were successful and carried them through another glass of champagne and the return to their seats, where he possessed himself of her hand and refused to release it for the remainder of the play.

When the last bow had been taken, they waited calmly in their seats as the crowd cleared the aisles, and she turned to him with a smile. "Whew! I've really been wrung out. Quite a catharsis, and I enjoyed every moment of it. Thank you for the loan of your handkerchief. A Kleenex may be disposably sanitary, but a handkerchief is much more satisfying to weep into. You know," she added thoughtfully, "a good cry under artistic stimulation is really remarkably invigorating."

"Good," he responded. "Then I won't have to warn you to brace yourself. First-night parties are invariably raucous and exhausting. The suspense is over and everyone treats him or herself to one hearty blowout before settling down, they hope, to the grind of a long-term run. Devon's parties," he finished dryly, "have a tendency to be more so than most."

She looked at him curiously. "You don't sound much enamored of cast parties."

"I'm generally not much of a social animal," he explained carefully. "Large groups of drunks irritate me, and I prefer to entertain on a more intimate basis." He gave her a wicked smile and laughed at her involuntarily shocked expression.

She regathered her composure and said as repressively as possible, "Then why are we going to this one?"

"Because I thought you might enjoy it," he said simply. She was immediately disarmed, all her resurgent wariness quashed by the sincerity of his words. He continued, "I thought you'd like to meet Devon and some of the other members of the cast, and I believe the playwright will be there too. He comes to first-nights but refuses to appear and take public bows. But it's up to you. If you'd rather, we can go dancing. . . ."

"Oh, no," she broke in hastily. "I'd really like to go to the party. I've admired Devon Harmon as an actor for quite a while."

He was very astute. "But not as a man?" he queried perceptively.

"Well . . ." She hesitated, but whether Devon was his friend or not she could only answer candidly. "No, I don't admire him as a man. I don't think much of men who prove their virility and masculinity by the number of women they take to bed. That should be a special relationship between a man and a woman, not a numbers contest. Unless his reputation is a total fabrication, he has more notches on his bedpost than Baron von Richthofen had air kills."

Breck surprised her. "Good!" he said with obvious satisfaction. "If you don't like him as a man, I won't have to warn him to keep away from you. Devon does have an abiding weakness for lovely women, and I wouldn't want to put his dresser to the trouble of having to disguise two black eyes for his stage appearances."

She thought he must be joking. He wasn't. She had only to look at the hard jut of his chin to realize he was perfectly serious. What was his, was his, and he didn't share.

The crowd had thinned and he guided her backstage. Quite a number of people greeted Breck cordially and he responded casually, congratulating them on the quality of the play. Andrea found it all fascinating and as they chatted with the second male lead while waiting for Devon to finish changing, she mused thoughtfully on the interesting process of metamorphosis the actors all underwent, from larger than life characters back into real-life human beings.

Breck duly introduced Devon before they all left to go to the hotel where the party was to be held. Andrea found him a most handsome animal, physically magnetic, but the use of her artist's fingers was not needed to lay bare his character. His eyes were dark and ardent, but his mouth had a lurking weakness. His charm was too well practiced and as a man he left her cold.

Breck must have been able to sense her perceptive summation of Devon, for, after watching their initial meeting with narrowed eyes, he suddenly relaxed and regarded the casually chatting pair amiably. Andrea was more than capable of keeping Devon in what Breck considered his place, and he seemed well content to let her do it. He did, however, tuck her hand in his arm once more, with a casually proprietorial air, when they all began to disperse before meeting again at the site of the party.

Devon watched this small byplay with an amused

and slightly rueful eye. Breck had found himself a real beauty, and it would have been interesting to have had a go at breaking through that intriguing air of reserve she wore like a cloak. A very tasty morsel, and he envied Breck first bite. He shrugged. His current leading lady was meal enough for any man.

Breck had been guilty of understatement, Andrea admitted silently. Devon's parties, if this were a representative sample, *were* more so than most. It seemed to be composed of a large number of wildly gesticulating, loudly talking people determined to consume tremendous amounts of liquor and very little else. The noise was just short of deafening, the haze of cigarette smoke steadily thickening, and the heat from the large number of bodies nearly stifled her. She had had enough.

Breck had been watching her closely and no sooner had she reached that conclusion than he bent to her and said quietly, "Had enough?"

She gave him a grateful smile. "Yes, please," she responded politely, a well brought up child. "It's gotten rather hot and noisy, hasn't it?"

"Yes, it has," he agreed smoothly. "We'll go somewhere quieter."

It wasn't what he said, and she really couldn't fault the way he said it, but suddenly Andrea had a flashing image of him as a Viking again, about to toss his spoils of war over his shoulder. Perhaps it was the way he had fended off the men who had tried to flirt with her, and there had been a considerable number of them.

She was an anomaly in this rather jaded, world-weary group, and she had drawn men's eyes like a magnet. Her serene reserve allied with her so obviously innocent enjoyment was irresistible, and a number of would-be gallants had tried their luck. At first Breck had seemed amused, content to allow Andrea to gently discourage without offense, but as the party had gotten louder and the advances more insistent, he had once again moved to make his claim obvious with a possessive arm about her waist.

No man with the smallest sense of self-preservation tries to take a juicy bone away from Cerberus, Andrea thought with amusement as the advances abruptly stopped.

There had been overtures toward Breck as well from the female segment of the party, but he had quickly, and in several instances rather brutally, made it clear that his only interest was in the woman who stood at his side. Even the leading lady, who was indeed a banquet to satisfy any man, received short shrift. She attempted to fling her arms around Breck's neck in exuberant greeting when she arrived on Devon's arm at the party, but was stopped by the firm grip of Breck's hands on her upper arms, which held her immobile several feet apart from him.

From the venomous look she shot at Andrea it was clear that she would not soon forget Andrea's witness of her humiliation, and several times during the evening Andrea intercepted seething glances directed her way. Breck had intercepted one of the glances and his face had become a hard mask.

It hadn't bothered Andrea in the least. She'd probably never see the woman again on a social basis, and her heavy-handed advances toward Breck had not touched Andrea at all. She was enjoying Breck's company, and it is never pleasant when one's escort for the evening pays marked attention to another woman, but she felt no deeply possessive instincts toward him.

Andrea was, if anything, rather leery of becoming closely involved with any man. The legacy of distrust, an inheritance from her father's behavior, made her chary of bestowing trust, and for her, where there was no trust, there could be no relationship closer and deeper than mild friendship, or so she told herself. The real truth was that no man had yet laid seige to her emotions. At a time when other girls were trying out their fledgling powers of fascination, she was earning a living and sitting beside her mother's rack of agony.

For the first two years after her mother's accident, she had dated no one. Too raw from grief and guilt, too tired from her hectic work schedule, she had hoarded her small amount of free time like a miser, using it to put her emotional house back in order. For a long time she had shunned men, tarring them with her father's brush, but finally her natural common sense and sturdy emotional balance had reasserted itself and she began to date again. With a wry mental smile she had told herself that men were people too, some good, some bad, and all to be taken on an individual basis, judged on their own special merits, not prejudged through the screen of her hatred of her father. Her emotional maturity was just about to catch up with her physical maturity. She was ripe . . . and very vulnerable.

Devon started to object when he saw them preparing to leave the party early, but one level-eyed look from Breck's blue eyes choked the words unsaid in his throat. No sneering insinuations blurted forth either. Breck was capable of ramming unwise words back down the unfortunate throats of those who uttered them and his markedly possessive air was warning enough that the lady was *his* lady.

The byplay went totally over Andrea's head The smoke and the noise had given her a headache that fresh air would cure, but while it lasted, nuances were beyond her. She appreciated Breck's immediate response to her unvoiced desire to leave but considered no implications. Since he had made it perfectly clear that the party was for her delectation, it was logical that they leave as soon as it ceased to be fun for her. She really didn't consider the insight that allowed him to know the instant she stopped enjoying herself. A more experienced woman would have.

The walk to the car cleared her head, blowing away the cobwebs of headache. She drew in deep lungfuls of crisp air and a sudden excess of joie de vivre overcame her natural dignity. She gave an impulsive skip, like a lamb gamboling in a spring meadow.

While Breck regarded her with almost paternal benevolence she tucked her arm confidingly through his and said with all the guileless candor of a child, "Thank you so much, Breck. The dinner was delicious, the play excellent, and the party a real experience. I enjoyed myself immensely." She smiled teasingly up at him before continuing in mock sorrowful tones, "And to think that I almost didn't come."

"And why didn't you almost come?" he asked indulgently, enjoying the play of the streetlights over her superb bone structure.

"Because I like to be asked, not told, even with such beautiful messengers," she responded, momentarily serious.

"Ah, but I only ask when I'm sure I'm going to get the answer I want. When I'm not sure the response will be favorable, I tell, not ask. It saves time."

"And when you tell, people do?" Her voice was still bantering, expecting him to laugh at the absurdity of a man *always* getting his own way.

"Yes, they do, little one."

She wrinkled her nose at him, still refusing to take him seriously. "Shall I tug my forelock, my lord, and sweep a humble curtsy?"

He chuckled at that. "You curtsy, men tug their forelocks. And then I sweep you up on my war-horse and carry you off to exercise my droit de seigneur, the fate of all lovely maidens who catch the eye of the lord of the manor."

"You're no lord of the manor. You're a Viking," she blurted out.

"That won't save you. Same fate, different surroundings. You're not prone to seasickness, are you?"

"Horribly!"

"Impossible. No mermaid was ever seasick. You can't escape your fate, my little siren of the sea."

Andrea was glad that they had reached the car. Breck helped her in and watched while she buckled her seat belt. He then locked and closed her door and went around to his own side of the car. She stretched over and unlocked his door before he could insert the key, and as he slid into his seat behind the wheel, she felt a sudden constriction in her throat. He was *so* big, so vitally masculine. She, unexpectedly and for the first time in her life, was sharply conscious of a man as a *man* in relation to herself as a *woman*.

Perhaps it was the conversation, lighthearted as it had been. In spite of dubbing him Viking, she suddenly had no trouble visualizing him as a blond Saxon/Norman amalgam, taking his pleasure from a village serf girl who caught his eye as he rode on tour of his demesne. Imperious Norman nose and clean-skinned jaw, blue-eyed, blond-haired Saxon coloring, and all the vigor of a hybrid.

She felt curiously flushed and hot, a warmth tingling through her veins. Perhaps it was the wine she'd drunk at dinner and at the party. She'd only had two glasses with dinner and another one at the party, holding it more for form's sake, but unconsciously sipping at it from time to time.

"Home?" he questioned her, breaking her train of thought into a million brittle slivers.

Her mouth opened, but the flippant "Home, James" wouldn't come. There was a sudden crackling tension between them. Home and . . . what? A chaste good-night kiss at the door? Suddenly she was as absurdly nervous as a girl on her first date. Will he or won't he, and if he does, what will I do?

Perhaps he took her silence for consent, or, in the dimness of the car, thought she had nodded acquiescence. He started the car and soon they were nearing familiar streets.

He parked the car and with unhurried smoothness got out and was around by her side, waiting for her to unlock her door. She did so and he helped her from the low seat, the warmth of his hand beneath her elbow a brand burning through the cloth to imprint the skin of her forearm with the length and strength of his fingers.

He slid an arm around her waist and they entered the elevator together, riding the clanking monster up and up. By the time they reached the sixth floor Andrea's throat was dry and she licked her lips nervously, once, twice.

What in the world was wrong with her? If Breck kissed her good night, what of it? Johnny had kissed her good night last week and would again when she went out with him. But Johnny is a boy, her mind whispered. Breck is a man and . . . they had reached her front door.

"Would—would you like some coffee?" she stammered. FOOL! her mind shrieked.

Breck smiled down at her. Her eyes were huge and uncertain and her lower lip trembled just a little. "I don't think I'd better," he responded dryly.

Her eyes grew larger, if that were possible. Disappointment and relief were inextricably mingled in eyes gone smoke soft and dark gray. "I—I—" she began.

"Little fool," he said with soft violence. "If I come in with you, I won't leave tonight, and you're not ready for that . . . yet."

Andrea gasped, as though she had just received two stiff fingers into her solar plexus. Shock, inexplicable excitement, relief, regret . . . she was a maelstrom of conflicting emotions and desires, and when Breck pulled her into his arms as though he couldn't help himself, she fell pliantly against him, trusting his powerful arms to be her support because her legs seemed suddenly jellyfish boneless.

She had never been in such intimate contact with the length of a male body. It was like leaning against a rock, hard, unyielding, yet burning with a heat which spoke of a molten core. Her warmly fleshed frame molded to his with the instinct of one piece of a jigsaw fitting into another.

He had no need to tilt her face up to meet his. Andrea's face lifted as the sunflower lifts to follow the god Apollo in his daily race across the sky. Her lips were closed but they parted beneath the touch of his, opening a gateway of exploration and delight.

53

Her arms crept up across his shoulders to wind around his neck, while his hands shaped and molded her, lying across the swell of her hips to pull her firmly against his lower body. She was only vaguely conscious of the intimacy of such contact because her attention was focused on the invasion of his mouth. She had known she was inexperienced, but he showed her just how much she had to learn.

She couldn't help herself. She responded to him with an untutored intensity that was to cost her a sleep-short night. If he had plundered, she had submitted, and even when she later castigated herself as all manner of idiot after he had gone, she could not lay the charge against him that he took what she was unwilling to give. Self-deception was not one of her faults, and she would not be able to excuse herself on those grounds. She had been a most willing participant, and if he had not allowed time for panic to set in, she would have agreed to . . . no, *urged!* . . . the final and complete ravishment of her senses.

As she lay in bed later that night, she went cold and shaking at the thought. She had been smug, strongly armored against overwhelming passion by her father's example. No man would enslave *her* as her mother had been enslaved, prisoner to a man's mastery of her desire. Andrea's passions would be closely reined, harnessed in the context of marriage, to a man she could trust. How bitter to learn she was human after all!

Breck had freed her mouth only to chase chills down the side of her neck to the soft hollows of her shoulder bones. In her dazed state it took awhile for the words he had whispered as his mouth trailed past her ear to form themselves into coherency.

"Perhaps I was mistaken," he had muttered. "Shall I indeed come inside with you?"

Passion shut off like a light switch clicking. Had he not spoken, had he just swept her into his arms and carried her into the dimly lit apartment, continuing to kiss and caress her with shattering, reason-blocking expertise, she might not now be lying in this bed, shivering and blessedly alone.

At her strangled "No!" he had paused, lifted his lips from the angle of her neck and shoulder for a moment, and then began to trail kisses back up the path he had just traced downward, intending to recapture her mouth and repair the damage his muttered words had torn in the fabric of sensual enchantment he was weaving around her.

To prevent the capture of her lips he so obviously intended, she buried her face in his shoulder, rolling her forehead back and forth against his collarbone in negation. He was too wise to force her head up. The strands of bewitchment are delicate and what begins as a small rift can rend the fabric beyond repair if too heavy a hand is used to mend it.

His hands began to stroke her back, gentling and soothing her, coaxing, not demanding. When she relaxed slightly, he eased her away from him and tilted her chin up to let her eyes meet his. He could not quite subdue the rueful twist to his smile, but it was a creditable effort nonetheless.

"Coffee would keep me awake all night and I have an important meeting to go to early tomorrow. Will you have dinner with me tomorrow night?"

Her instincts had urged an immediate and re-sounding "No!" but the husky "Yes" popped out instead. He had asked, not told, but the result was the same. He had given her no chance to back out.

55

At his gesture she had handed him the key and he had unlocked the door. He gave her back the key and, grasping her shoulders gently, he dropped a kiss on her forehead, turned her about, and propelled her inoooapably into her living room. His voice came softly over her shoulder, but she could tell ho had not entered after her.

"I'll pick you up tomorrow night at seven. Lock the door behind me."

The door clicked shut behind him, but he didn't move away at once. When she made no move to obey him, he tapped softly on the door and reiterated through the panels, "Lock it, Andrea."

She hastily obeyed and he moved away, his firm footsteps echoing down the hall. Andrea fled to her bedroom before the elevator began its descent.

Now she lay in bed, her eyes riveted to the sketch, trying to pull from it the answers she wanted from its living model. She put it down, picked up her sketch block, and drew another. Perhaps she could now see deeper into the complexities of his personality.

The second sketch was done. She held the two up to compare them. There were differences, to be sure. More humor glinted in the eyes, but to her dismay, more ruthless purpose firmed the lines of the face of her second sketch. This man looked at what he wanted and was prepared to take it. Patience, a quality she had overlooked before, was there, but when patience was ended and still his will was thwarted, he would take. More of the primitive sensuality showed than in the previous sketch, but perhaps that was because she came fresh from its experience. It had always been implicit.

It was the portrait of the Viking still, making no

commitments save those of the flesh, ready to go a-roving after lust was assuaged. In modern terms, her mouth quirked wryly, a man for affairs, not binding commitments.

How ironic! How sadly similar . . . she and her mother. Had she learned nothing from that bitter lesson, that she would so easily fall into the arms of a man who would take and take and never give her anything but passion?

When the body craves and the mind denies, the resultant conflict can be fierce and prolonged. Andrea's body, newly wakened to passion, was not prone to go meekly back to innocence. Impossible to spit out the bite from the fruit of the tree of knowledge . . . the flavor lingers seductively on the taste buds. But in the end the weight of experience, her mother's experience, told. Her mind mastered her rebellious body. She would go to dinner with Breck tomorrow night, but no more. She was achingly aware of her vulnerability where Breck was concerned, and she was not too proud to find safety in flight. No charge of cowardice, no sweet persuasion would move her. Three years of discipline and many more of watching the pain a faithless husband can inflict had done their job. Her body would obey her mind in this matter!

The next morning she resumed her routine. If her face was a little drawn and her eyes held more than a touch of frosty bleakness, it could be laid to a late night partying. Her mind might have won, but the body wasn't going to yield a bloodless victory. She had slept badly and had woken more than once, twisted in the sheets and hugging her pillow in a death grip.

She checked the painting and found it dry enough

57

to transport if she was careful. She inspected it critically and even her currently captious eye could find no fault. Andrea had achieved exactly the effect she had striven for and just now that achievement was made savorless by the deep longing for the taste of one man's mouth and the hard strength of that one man's arms . . . a man she should not, would not have.

She took the painting with her that afternoon and the delight in her mother's face was reward enough.

"It's the best you've ever done, Andrea, dear," Jeanne's thin voice said quietly. "I can smell the fresh earth and hear the breeze rustle the leaves. When I look at it, I am free from this prison of a room and body for a while. Remember the long walks we used to take when you were a little girl and that grassy little hill that we always stopped on to eat our picnic lunch? When we were finished, you used to roll down the hill, over and over."

Andrea laughed gently, falling deliberately into the mood of drowsy reminiscence. More and more her mother seemed to escape her current dreary life into the happier, pain-free past. "I remember," she agreed softly. "And remember the one time you decided to roll down the hill yourself? Those two prim school teachers and their nature class came along and caught you. So disapproving and sour . . . I bet they were just jealous because they were too inhibited to try it themselves."

Jeanne grew suddenly serious. She looked at her daughter as she sat beside the high hospital bed. She stretched out a fleshless hand and Andrea grasped it warmly with her young, supple, clever fingers. Jeanne's hand was dry and cold, unable to grasp anything strongly anymore, even to hold on to her life, which was slipping relentlessly through her strengthless fingers.

"Andrea, my very dear daughter. The best thing that ever came into my life was given to me when I flouted a convention the world cherishes. I have never regretted what I did. I want you to know that." She paused, seeming to search for words and strength.

"I know this has been cruelly hard on you, darling. Your father . . ." Andrea's face assumed a masklike rigidity, but her mother pressed on, rather desperately. "Your father is not an easy man to love. I know his faults . . . who better . . . but the habit of love is strong, and I have loved him from the time he was the boy next door. Perhaps, if at the first I had acted differently, our lives might all have taken a better path, but by the time you came along the pattern was set and he and I were locked into our assigned roles. You were my small miracle, you know. I loved you from the first time I held your warm tiny body next to my heart, and you washed away the bitterness that lurked, corroding, in my heart. I forgave him much when he gave me you."

"Oh, Mother, please don't!" Andrea's voice was muffled, her face buried in the bedside. "I can't bear what he's done to you. I cannot love him, even for your sake."

Jeanne patted and stroked her daughter's bent head. "I know, my dear." Her voice was sad. "Through his own willful, weak actions he lost one of the greatest gifts life offers us, the unstinting love of his child. If you could have known him as a child . . . you were very like him, bright, eager for life . . . he didn't always content himself with the dross."

She rested for a moment and then continued, "I

have loved him for so long . . . Andrea, listen to me. He does not hurt me anymore. I . . . I pity him now. I've paid and learned from my mistakes, but he is still the greedy child, grabbing at pleasure and watching it melt, insubstantial and unfulfilling, through his hands. If you cannot love him, at least don't hate him anymore, for your own sake. Pity him instead. To hate him will only hurt *you*. It will warp you. Hate corrodes and twists the one who carries it within him like a cancer. You can't accept joy if you are filled with hatred. Learn from your father's and my mistakes, my very dear. Don't let our example make you afraid to love, to trust. You may get hurt . . . life is painful . . . but you will also find joy. I want that for you, Andrea. I want it very badly."

Andrea was sobbing softly. She wasn't a small child anymore, able to take her small tragedies to her mother and have them all made well. Her tragedies were big ones now and there was no one to take them to. Somewhere, somehow, she had to find the inner strength to bear them herself and to justify this woman's faith in her. They were silent for a long while after that, the woman who was at the end of her life and the young girl just beginning hers.

Finally Andrea was able to raise her head. Jeanne was looking peacefully at the picture Andrea had brought and hung, for the moment all tension and suffering in abeyance. She turned her head and smiled sweetly, a glimpse of her old beauty flickering into life. "And now, Andrea, dear, tell me about your evening last night. How was the play, and is Devon Harmon really as handsome as he seems from his pictures? Do you like this Breck Carson and—"

"Stop! Halt! Cease and desist!" Andrea was laughing at the sudden flood of questions. "I've already

60

forgotten what the first question was. One at a time, please, if you really want them answered."

She went on to describe the play and party in detail, what the various personalities she had met had said and done (some of it) and her impressions of some of the great and near-great when met in the flesh. She talked determinedly of everyone and everything except Breck.

She should have known her perceptive mother would not let such blatant evasion pass. The quiet "And what of Breck Carson, Andrea? Do you like him?" jolted her eloquence to a halt in midspate.

Andrea thought faster than she ever had in her life. This had to be done just right. She allowed a smile to crinkle the corners of her eyes. "Well, that's sort of hard to say. Breck is too dynamic a person to say you merely like him. I enjoyed my evening and he was a most attentive escort, but I think a steady diet of him would be . . . ah . . . overwhelming. He's rather exhausting." She continued carefully. "I *am* having dinner with him tonight, but then he's flying off to some big meeting and I don't imagine I'll see much of him for a while after that."

There, not a lie in the bunch. Her mother had an uncanny ear for the lie. She always had, probably from listening to so many of her husband's, Andrea thought cynically.

The rest of the visit went smoothly. Andrea left a bit earlier than usual because her mother was very tired, and she knew she could make good use of the time, preparing herself for the evening. There was no anticipation, only dread. If she could, she would like to sleep through the whole thing and wake up the next morning with it all behind her, like some nightmare that would eventually fade with the dawn and full awakening. Breck wasn't going to be easy to get over, but the sooner she started, the better for her.

CHAPTER THREE

Promptly at seven that imperious double knock echoed through the door. As before, she opened the door and gestured him inside, but this time she didn't offer him her hand, nor did she stand where he could pull her into his embrace. He noted her caution and his mouth twitched while a glint appeared in his eyes.

"There's no need to stand so far away, Andrea. It won't make any difference. If I decide to kiss you, I'll just come get you." He grinned, but she could see he wasn't joking.

She decided it would be more dignified to ignore that sally, and besides, she couldn't think of a good comeback. "Would you like a drink before we go?" She was the poised hostess, and his mouth twitched again.

"Yes, I believe I would," he answered her quietly.

She started to move toward and past him to the kitchen, where she kept the few bottles of liquor for her occasional guests and the wine she herself preferred when she infrequently drank. "What would you care for?" she began to say.

As she came level with him, he swept her into his arms and chuckled, "You! How obliging of you to come to me. It saved me the trouble of coming to get you." He kissed her with leisurely thoroughness.

When he released her, Andrea could only sputter, "You said you wanted a drink!"

He laughed, the first one she'd ever heard from him. It was a very nice laugh, she thought wistfully, deep and rumbling and uninhibited but not booming. "You're the only thing intoxicating I need, honey. Come on, it's time to go if you expect to go out for dinner tonight. I'd just as soon stay here, but I did promise to feed you."

They had dinner at a different restaurant from the one they had gone to the night before, but the food and service were equally good. It seemed that Breck had only to lift an eyebrow and a waiter would materialize at his elbow. He seemed intent on plying her with wine and Kobe beef until she wondered aloud if he were trying to get her either too drunk or too stuffed with food to move when he made advances.

That marvelous laugh rang out again and the look he gave her warned that she trod on dangerous ground. Such suggestive bandying opened avenues of speculation she must keep closed, although, she mused, it wasn't necessary to put ideas in his head. Every look he gave her told her that they were already there.

After they had chosen their dinner menu and selected personally which of the superb thick steaks were to be grilled to perfection, he didn't really take his eyes off of her for the rest of the evening. When a waiter appeared, ready to carry out his slightest command, he gave his orders without shifting his attention from her face.

For all her dread of the scene that was bound to ensue at the conclusion of the evening, Andrea found him easy to talk to. He had definite opinions on a wide range of subjects without being opinionated. He could make her laugh, and did, and he held her spellbound with stories of his summers at lumber camps.

Deserted by his parents when he was a young boy, Breck had gone through a very rebellious period, passing through a series of foster homes so quickly "they barely had time to learn my name. I escaped being remanded to custody of the local reform school only because I finally ran up against a foster parent who was bigger than I was. He literally walloped the daylights out of the seat of my pants. Then he sat me down and told me that if my eventual destination was to be state prison, I was well started. If, however, I wanted to make something of myself and prove that I wasn't as worthless as the parents who had abandoned me, he'd show me the way."

Breck's voice was sad. "He's dead now, but before he died, he convinced me to buckle down to studying. Then he arranged summer jobs where I could use my strength and work off some of the normal frustrations any teen-age boy has with hard, grinding labor. It was just what I needed. In the lumber camps nobody cared about my background. They accepted me for what I was and the work I could do. I earned my place among them by the sweat of my brow, literally."

When he began to tell her about his background, Andrea had writhed inside. Don't, she had wanted to say. Please don't. What good will it do me to see behind the outer skin, to know why you are the way you are today? Will it change the way I feel about you or only deepen my feelings, make it that much harder to forget you, as I must?

She could have wept for that little boy who

65

thought himself worthless because his parents had abandoned him, and would have proved it to the world if a wise, practical man had not shown him another way. She would weep later for the strong man as she strove to cut him from her life, severing with surgical brutality all the emotions and longings that already bound the image of him in her heart.

He had captured her hand across the table and was stroking the back of her palm with his thumb, distractingly, as he talked. "I finally evolved a workable philosophy from all that," he concluded. "Your parents, whoever and whatever they are, give you life and, if you're lucky, a good base to start out from, but what you make of yourself, in the final analysis, depends at last on your own abilities and the use you make of them. If you have rotten parents, you start out with a handicap, but one that can be overcome."

The look he gave her was somehow significant, but Andrea was unwilling to decipher it, so concerned was she with combating this man's heady and growing attraction. She turned the conversation to less personal topics and he followed her lead, but a shade of disappointment flashed across his face so swiftly, she wasn't even sure she had seen it.

When the leisurely dinner was finished, they sat for a while over coffee, engrossed in conversation. Andrea was enjoying herself thoroughly, living for the moment, forgetting what was to come, but when Breck began to probe again, as he had the night they had met, she snapped back into her defensive shell.

"I don't talk or think about my father, Breck, if I can possibly avoid it." Her eyes had lost their gray-velvet softness and paled with an icy sheen. "What he is and what he does now cannot affect me anymore. What damage he can do has been done and is past mending. His business life was never my concern, and his personal life doesn't interest me in the least. He'll find his own damnation, and those he'd have taken with him are free of him now."

He was taken aback by her vehemence. He had known there was no love lost on her part, but this depth of feeling went beyond simple jealousy or moral outrage. He'd not yet received the complete dossier on Thomas, but he'd have it by tomorrow to take with him for study, or someone's head would roll.

"All right, Andrea," he agreed peaceably, but the damage was already done. She was tense and nervy again, all accord between them disrupted. When she requested that he take her home, he agreed. He had the feeling that she would be capable of taking a taxi alone if he didn't, and while he wouldn't have let her do it, he didn't fancy having to sling her over his shoulder to prevent it either. There was plenty of time to find the key to her behavior. It obviously lay somewhere in the relationship between Thomas and herself, and once armed with more facts about Devlin Thomas, he'd know the best way to approach her without perpetually running afoul of the minefields which guarded the subject.

He didn't try to touch her as they walked back to the car, wisely, because Andrea was ready to react to his slightest advance with the ferocity of a young wildcat. Any mention of her father had a deleterious effect on her temper and had only reinforced her decision to break off her developing relationship with Breck. Her mind was in full ascendancy and she used the weapon—her father, and Breck's probing about him—to augment her determination to subdue her

67

treacherous body's yearnings and awakened hungers.

As before, they stood outside her door, but this time Breck didn't try to kiss her. He waited until she unlocked the door, and as she turned back to thank him for the meal, he forestalled her words.

"Don't say good night yet, Andrea. I'm coming in for that cup of coffee, and there's something inside that belongs to me."

She looked closely at him, trying to fathom what was behind his words. If he was giving her fair warning that he intended to seduce her, she might have a nasty surprise for him. Right now she was proof against his lovemaking, and the only way she'd succumb to him tonight would be if he raped her, and *that* wasn't his style.

"All right, Breck. A cup of coffee it is."

Now it was his turn to eye her closely. She had agreed easily, but he suddenly realized that somehow she was completely impervious to him. She had moved to some remote distance, though her body was still enticingly close and he could smell the delicious scent of her. It was the same feeling he'd had when he danced with her the first time. She had deliberately cut off all sensual awareness of him as a man. It irritated him, because he had held her in his arms and knew she was alive and warm, exciting to him as no other woman had ever been.

Andrea left him in the living room, standing before the painting, marveling again at the technique that had made the coy mermaid come to life. When she came back, bearing the coffee and impedimenta on a tray, he was still in the same position.

She smiled slightly and remarked, "If you try too hard, your eyes will start to cross from eyestrain.

Mermaids are elusive creatures at best. Let the poor girl swim away to the depths where she's happiest, Breck. Your coffee's poured and getting cold."

"Mermaids are trappable," he responded as he obediently picked up his cup and sat down on the couch. "It just takes the right kind of bait."

Andrea kicked off her shoes and tucked her feet up under herself as she sat on the couch. She regarded him thoughtfully over the rim of her own cup. "And just what bait would you use to trap a mermaid? Jewels, pieces of eight?" she scoffed gently. "She can get those herself from the bottom of the ocean floor. I think it would have to be very special bait to tempt a mermaid, to make her endure the pain of breathing air like sharp knives through her gills and walk slowly and painfully on dry land after she had been able to glide through silken waters with the freedom of a bird on air. Mermaids know their fate on dry land, you know. Word got passed around after the Little Mermaid came to grief. Mermaids were never too proud to learn from another's experience, and they have long memories as a breed."

Her face was bitter and sad as she looked down some dark memory of her own. He would have given much just then to be able to read her mind. She was warning him off. It was unmistakable, and the memory that lay sad shadows over her face held the key he needed.

"I won't tell you what bait I plan to use. You might warn the mermaid, and then she'd get away from me. I don't intend for that to happen. I've wanted her from the moment I laid eyes on her, and I'll have her." He kept to the metaphor they both employed to cloak the direct meaning and watched her face grow grave.

"Have you thought about the mermaid at all? How she feels, I mean? You're prepared to take her from her natural element, to force new experiences on her that she may not want." She looked directly at him for the first time, her gray eyes questioning and pleading. "Trophy fishing is a cruel sport, Breck. A mermaid deserves a better fate than to be a dusty symbol hung up on some hunter's game room wall."

It was the only appeal she would ever make to him and she knew before she made it that it was useless. Futile to hope for mercy to soften that warrior's face. Her fingers had not lied. There was no compassion in those Viking-blue eyes, which met her own in silent battle.

Well, as you will, she thought dispiritedly. Let us play out the script to the black and bitter end.

"You said that there was something in this apartment that belonged to you, Breck. Would you like to tell me what it is now that you've had your coffee?" She put her cup down, half finished, and waited patiently for him to make the next move.

Her armor was back in place. For a moment she had let it drop and he had again glimpsed the woman, enchanting and desirable, and his determination to have her was intensified. She fired his blood and he was having a hard time keeping his hands off her. No man had ever had her. It was obvious—she might as well have worn a placard with VIRGIN splashed across it—and perhaps a good portion of her fears were directly attributable to that fact. That and a fastidious unwillingness to engage in casual affairs such as her father obviously cluttered his life with.

He grinned inwardly. The affair he had planned with her would have nothing *casual* about it! She'd be able to send a man mad with pleasure, and he'd damn well make sure to take her with him when he went. Oh, no! He'd have his mermaid yet, warm and willing in his bed, no trophy on a wall. Whatever had given her that idea in the first place? Did she think all he wanted from her was a one-night stand? Oh, little mermaid, how little you know of men and yourself, to think that a man could be satisfied to have you once and then forget you, walking away without a backward glance. I don't plan to leave you after just one night. I want more of you than that!

No sign of his inner musings appeared on his face, and when he spoke, she looked at him in surprise. He said, "What kind of frame had you planned to use on my picture?"

"*Your* picture?" Involuntarily she looked up at the sea scene on the wall behind them before looking at him in bewilderment. "Frame?"

"I told you I wanted it," he said patiently, but to her, obscurely. "I bought it this morning from Mrs. Carrington. Or, to be precise, I bought her right to buy it. I understand she had paid you a deposit but not the full price."

He half turned on the couch, felt in his back pocket, and pulled out his wallet. He opened it and took out a check, made out in her name, and handed it to her. She stared down at it blankly, then back up at him.

"Sylvia sold you her picture? This morning?" She couldn't seem to take it in. She would have sworn . . . He must have offered Sylvia an exorbitant amount of money.

"But you could have commissioned one for yourself if you liked my work so much. There was no need to let Sylvia hold you up. She wouldn't have let that picture go cheaply, and it isn't worth what I'm sure

71

you had to pay, including this." She gestured vaguely at the check, which lay in her lap.

"I set my own values," he responded with more than a touch of arrogance. "It's worth more than I paid and I wanted *that* painting. You price your work too cheaply, Andrea. Given the right exposure, you could command quadruple the price you ask now. You shouldn't sell piecemeal. Gather enough canvases for a showing, let a reputable gallery set up the show for you, and I guarantee that you'll more than cover the expenses the gallery will charge, as well as allow your private sales to skyrocket, both in demand and price."

"I don't have time to paint for a show. If I manage to turn out four or five canvases a year, I'm doing well. I earn my living, Breck. Right now serious painting has to take a backseat. I . . . I have other commitments."

"Commercial art!" His tone was contemptuous. "It's a crime against your talent. I'm certainly no expert, but even I can see the worth of what you can do."

She was getting angry now. She knew as well, no, better than he, that she should be painting seriously full-time, and she knew, as he did not, why she could not yet paint as she desired. Too soon, all too soon she would be free to paint, and the cost of her freedom brought tears to her eyes and a sharp lump to her throat. In her pain she struck out at him verbally.

"What I do is none of your concern, Breck. You can have your painting next week. I'll give you the name of the shop where I get my frames and you can pick out the one you like for yourself. I'll arrange it beforehand. Just tell Kevin which one you want and he'll frame it, no charge. It's included in the cost of the painting."

Andrea was being deliberately offensive, but she couldn't seem to stop. It was insanity to bait Breck this way, but the consequences didn't deter her. For too long, too many years, she had exercised unnatural control and she was reaching her limits at long last. With tremendous effort she looked directly at him, her face strained and masklike.

"The evening is over, Breck. Thank you for the dinner. I'd like you to leave now."

She rose from the couch and stood looking down at him, waiting for him to rise so that she could escort him to the door. The check had drifted to her feet, forgotten, and when she found it the next day, there was part of a footprint across it where one of them had trod upon it.

"I'd like to see my painting again before I go, since I can't have it until next week." Breck rose to his feet, and she had to tilt her head far back to meet his eyes, because she was barefooted, her shoes discarded by the couch.

"I'm sorry. That's not possible." She *was* sorry. If it would make him leave, she would have shown him anything.

His eyes narrowed. "Why isn't it possible? You said it was finished, and even if it's not dry enough to move, I won't be touching it. I just want to look at it." He started toward the studio door.

Her voice stopped him. "You can't see it now, because it's not here."

"Where is it, Andrea?" His voice was quietly dispassionate.

He never calls me Andy, she thought irrelevantly. I wonder why not? Aloud, she answered him precise-

73

ly. "It's hanging on the wall facing my mother's bed, in her room at the Grayson Convalescent Home. I always leave my newest picture with her for a while after it's completed. It gives her something different to look at besides four hospital walls. I took it there today, as soon as it was dry enough to move. You can have it next week."

"Your mother? I thought your mother was dead. Your father—"

He found it hard to believe that such a bitter laugh could come from such a lovely mouth. "My father?" She finished the implied sentence. "No, my father doesn't advertise that his wife is still alive. But she is! My father will have to wait awhile to be totally free of her. But it's just a legal formality, after all . . . dust to dust and all that. She died to him a little over three years ago, and he plays the merry widower very well."

"Three years ago . . . when you were eighteen." Puzzle pieces were clicking into place rapidly now.

"One week after I was eighteen, to be precise. My mother was crippled in a car accident. After they'd done all they could for her in the hospital, she was moved to the nursing home and she's been there ever since, and will be . . ."

"And you left your father's house." He said it quietly, but it was a statement of fact, not a question.

"Yes."

"Was he driving?"

"No. But he drove her."

He considered that ambiguous statement and wondered if she'd enlarge on it. He looked at her face and knew she wouldn't.

"Is she paralyzed?" It seemed a reasonable question to him, but she flinched as though he had struck

74

her across the face, and that biting, throat-tearing laugh, which was no laugh, ripped from her throat again.

"Paralyzed? No, she's not paralyzed. I wish to God she was! If she was, at least the pain would be gone. She can't walk, but she has feeling in her legs and torso. You can't imagine. I've heard her *screaming* from the feeling! Her spine was fractured beyond all mending, and they pulled her back from death to endure three years of living hell."

She had almost forgotten he was present. Three years of torment spewed forth in her husky voice. "I go every day. On her good days, we talk and I see the mute agony in her eyes and graven ever deeper in the lines of her face. On her bad days, I watch the tears that are forced from her eyes and listen to the moans that blurt from her lips, no matter how tightly she tries to close them."

Appalled, he said, "But there are drugs. Surely they can sedate her!"

Flatly she informed him, "Continued dosage strong enough to take away the pain, or even most of it, would kill her, and no doctor will take that responsibility. I would do it for her, if she asked me, but she will not. So they keep her balanced on the sharp razor edge, as they have for three years. Enough drugs to keep the pain from being totally unendurable, but not enough to release her. If she had been a weaker woman, she would have died long ago, but she is . . . was . . . strong and so she lingers."

"I'm sorry, Andrea. It's inadequate, but I'm sorry."

She looked right at him, but she didn't see him. "I hate my father, Breck. Before . . . before her accident I disliked him, but now I hate him. My mother tells me not to hate him, but I do. He should be in that bed. Perhaps, when she is dead and at peace at last, I can forget him. Not forgive him, but forget him. Blot him out as though he never existed."

Long rolling shudders were shaking her slender body and her arms were wrapped tightly around her waist. She was still staring straight ahead, unseeing. He could see her face and her eyes were blazing hot and icy cold, but she was not crying. If her mother was in hell, had been for three years, Andrea had been right there with her. It was a crushing burden for such a slender back to bear.

He moved close to her and put his hands on her shoulders, intending to hold her close, to comfort her. She went board rigid and jerked away from him.

"No!" she gasped. Andrea knew she dared not accept comfort from him. She longed to, longed to let that broad chest block out the world and to have those muscular arms enfold her. She wanted desperately to be cradled and comforted. Breck had cracked her shell as only he seemed to be able to do at will, and she could not bring herself to trust him to give her only the human warmth of a body to lean against.

"Go away, Breck." Her eyes were pleading, piteous. "Go away and let me find what peace I can tonight. You've done enough damage to me with your prodding and poking. I've said things to you that I've never said aloud to another human being, and such things are better left unspoken. They do not purge or cleanse. They only sear the mouth that says them."

"Sit back down on the couch, Andrea. I'm not going to leave you while you're still upset. I won't touch you, but I'm going to get you a drink, a brandy

76

if you have some, and I'm going to watch you drink it. And I'm going to have one myself," he finished twistedly.

There was no help for it. Andrea knew it now. The whole farce was going to be played out to the ghastly end. She had hoped to put it off until she had recovered from this devastating storm of emotion that had so recently raged through her, but he would not let her be. She would drink the brandy, which she loathed, regain her fragile calm, and then another storm was going to break over her achingly weary head.

Perhaps it was better this way, she thought as she moved to sit on the couch as he had directed. She leaned her head back against the wall and closed her eyes. Breck was opening and closing cabinet doors, looking for the store of liquor and the glasses. Let him. The longer it took him, the more time she had to pull herself back together. Perhaps it was cowardly to hope to put off the final confrontation, but it had to be done, so why not cap a perfectly awful day with a really massive explosion?

That was a rhetorical question if ever there was one. There was no way to put it off. Breck was adept at pushing her into corners. He'd been doing it ever since she'd danced with him . . . before even, because she knew he'd sent her father over to bring Johnny and her back to the head table. Her father would never have approached her like that in a public place, with one of his women in tow.

Devlin wouldn't trust her to preserve a polite facade. She'd never made a scene before, except for the time she had told him what she thought of him after her mother's accident. There had only been the two of them present at the house while she was packing to leave, but he'd never risk a confrontation like that one again.

Breck had found the brandy and glasses. Her glass was half full but his own was nearly brimming. It was the only indication that the scene a short while ago had affected him as well. His face was calm and a little remote; his eyes a darker blue than usual, perhaps. He handed her the glass, his fingers touching hers only briefly, releasing it as soon as he was sure she had a firm grasp.

He didn't take his eyes from her face, watching her as she sipped and made a face and sipped again. She really hated the taste of brandy. It hit her stomach with a dull thud and burned. She set the glass down half finished and said, "I'm calm now. I don't want any more brandy."

It was true. Resignation had made her calm. She supposed it must be akin to the feeling when sentence has been passed and the firing squad is inevitable. Resignation, dull acceptance, because the emotions have been wrung dry, and a readiness to have done with it. All hope gone and only grim determination to carry one through with some semblance of dignity.

"I have to fly back to New York tomorrow afternoon. I'll be gone a week." Breck's words were choppy, the sentences abrupt, spurting forth under pressure. "I have to go. Have lunch with me before I leave."

Here it was. She drew in a deep breath and let it out slowly, soundlessly. "No, Breck." Gentle but implacable. The refusal was for more than lunch, and they were both aware of it.

"Why?" His face was drawn, beginning to grow stern with anger. Two lines had appeared between nostril edge and the outer corners of his mouth, silent betrayal of the control he was exerting.

"I owe you no reasons, Breck." Her voice was still quiet and she met his blue eyes squarely.

"Don't you, Andrea?" His voice rasped slightly. His control did not equal hers. "Are you afraid of me? Or your own desires? You can't deny that kiss last night. You may be a coward, but you're not a liar."

"Thank you," she flared with heavy irony. "I'm not ashamed of it, Breck. You call me a coward and it's true. I'm attracted to you and I responded to you. I won't deny it." Her head lifted proudly and still she faced him eye to eye. "But it won't go any further than that, because I won't let it. It won't, and nothing you do or say will change that."

He started to speak, but she interrupted him ruthlessly. "Can you promise me that you would be content with a platonic relationship?" Her laugh held a touch of genuine amusement at the expression on his face. "No, I can see that idea holds no appeal for you."

She leaned forward, hands on knees. Determined to make herself perfectly understood, she spaced her words clearly and with chill precision. "I will not, will never have an affair with you. There are reasons you don't know and I don't propose to tell you that make me very sure of that. But you do attract me . . . see how honest I am being? An honest coward. I *don't* trust myself around you so I won't *be* around you. Call me coward, call me craven. You can't goad me and you won't change my mind. I have all the misery I can handle in my life right now and I am not about to deliberately set myself up for more. I am a coward, but I'm not suicidal."

She stood and faced him bravely. "Please go now, Breck." Her words were little more than a husky whisper. She was at the end of her strength. "Throw the mermaid back. Take her off that cruel hook and let her swim away to her safe, dark depths."

It was an appeal that should have cracked a stone. Not a muscle flickered in the mask of his face. Had she sketched him just then, there would have been nothing but a cruel, blank mask, no feelings exposed, no pity. Only his eyes were alive and they blazed with a terrible anger.

She was really going to do it! This slender, woman-fragile girl was going to turn him out of her life. Deny him. Not see him ever again except perhaps a chance meeting on the street. Pride of manhood and other emotions he would not name rose up in overwhelming rebellion. The fingers of his hands clenched spasmodically.

Andrea wasn't looking at him now. The last burst of emotion completed her exhaustion. She had nothing left in reserve. She had made her appeal and if he chose to disregard it, she was defenseless. She stood before him in the eternal posture of the captive woman, head bowed for the yoke of submission. She was crying at last, slow, silent tears dripping in a steady stream. She didn't sob or make a sound, wasn't even really aware of the moisture on her cheeks.

He picked her up, holding her tightly in case she struggled, but she lay supine in his arms. He sat back down on the couch, arranged her comfortably in his lap, and began to kiss and caress her.

She was a pliable wax doll and her lips had all the exciting possibilities of a mannequin. No kiss of either tenderness or passion had the power to move her or make her respond. Even when his hand slid inside the neck of her dress to cup her breast, tracing the nipple bud with his thumb, she lay quiescent, spent.

It was passive resistance at its worst. He was defeated. She had locked all her responses behind a glass wall and nothing he could do now could move or reach her. If he stripped her naked and laid her on the rug to take her as a marauding Norseman might have taken a war prize in some convenient ditch, she would lie flaccid beneath him.

He lifted his mouth from hers, his hand from her full, warm breast and cursed. "All right, Andrea. You've won. No man enjoys making love to a rag doll."

He tilted her face back so he could see it clearly. Her eyes were closed, the steady tears leaking from beneath the tear-spiked lashes, but had her eyes opened at that moment, she would have been puzzled by the expression of intense and awful agony that carved lines in his face. Her eyes stayed closed. She did not see.

He looked at her for a long, silent moment and then put her aside. He stood up, looming over her. He could not leave her there on the couch. Her pallor bespoke total exhaustion and she might well lie there uncomfortably all night. He scooped her up, found the bedroom, grimaced at the single bed, and pulled back the spread, one-handed.

When she was tucked, dress and all, beneath the covers, he said quietly, "Andrea, look at me." Her heavy, reddened lids lifted slowly, so slowly, and she focused on him painfully.

"Good-bye, Andrea."

He turned and walked from the room, switching off the light as he went.

Andrea heard him go. Heard him cross the floor,

81

open the front door, and close it behind himself. The muted rumble of the elevator came next, dying away into empty, echoing silence. That was the way she felt inside. Empty. Echoing. The last quiet "good-bye" was a slowly fading echo and reecho somewhere in that vast loneliness.

She was hollow inside. It was a strange sensation, as though her outer skin stretched over nothing but a black vacuum. Cold and dark and empty. No pain, no joy, no tears, no laughter. Numb. The feeling extended itself into her head. She fainted.

Sometime during the faint she slipped insensibly into slumber. When she woke the next morning, it was hard to open her eyes. They were glued stickily shut, as though someone had tied her upper and lower eyelashes together in knots. She stumbled, half-blindly, to the bathroom and ran cool water over her hands, lifting cupped handfuls to splash over her face. The chill shock of the water drove the muzziness away and she lifted a dripping face to inspect it in the mirror. Ugh! If she hadn't already been depressed, the sight of her own face would have made her so.

She remembered it all. There was no comforting amnesia, so beloved of the novelists as a deus ex machina. She had sent Breck away and he had gone, without a backward glance.

What she had done had been right. It had been necessary, but it was like tearing herself in half. She had not known how *much* he meant to her until she sent him away . . . and he went. Futile *if only*'s chased madly through her tired brain. *If only* he'd refused to go. But he didn't. *If only* he'd said, "I can't lose you. I love you. Marry me!" But he hadn't.

He hadn't, she told herself drearily. She had ac-

82

complished what she had set out to do and now it was necessary to get on with the business of living. Just why escaped her right now, but presumably habit would carry her through. Habit turned on the shower and kept her under it until she emerged, drenched and shivering, but somewhat more wide awake. Habit made the coffee, which was all her churning stomach would accept.

It was one of her mother's very bad days, so Andrea need make no excuses for her pallor and grim-jawed silence. The nurses whispered sympathetically behind her back. They had all admired her devotion and unflagging solicitude, her inventive patience and her productive compassion for the other patients. They were sorry to see the strain and heart-wrenching business of watching a loved one slowly die lay its dimming pall over her normal vitality.

It took her mother three days to pull herself partway back up the dark slope she had slid so far down. Andrea had been by her bed long past regular visiting hours, holding the weightless, stick-boned hand. She wasn't trying to hold death back, far from it. She could ask no kinder release for her beloved mother. She merely gave what poor comfort she could, projecting warmth and love through that clasp, young hand to old.

She stayed each night until those fleshless fingers relaxed their frail hold on consciousness, no matter how late it was. She could have stayed past midnight, if necessary, with the nurses' blessing. A doctor's order was not needed to allow her the freedom of her mother's room. The nurses would have brought a bed in for her had she requested it, but she sat upright, hour after hour, in a hardbacked chair to help her stay awake.

By the end of the third day her mother had come back, as far as she was able, one more time. As Jeanne waxed, Andrea waned. She had not regained her accustomed color and she had lost weight. The hours by her mother's bed had left her with far too much time for reflection and she had gone over and over her few memories of Breck until they were threadbare.

She had heard nothing from him, nor did she expect to, and she tried to discipline herself into believing it was all for the best. She slept very badly and ate poorly and, if she was honest with herself, she had to admit it was due in part to concern over her mother's condition. But by far Breck and thoughts of him gave her the sleepless nights and stole her appetite. She was miserable and it showed.

Even when her mother rallied, Andrea continued to look haunted, and the nurses began eyeing her with concern. Andrea resorted to makeup, using more blusher than usual to put some color, artificial or not, in her cheeks.

On Wednesday night she took down the painting Breck had bought, although she had not yet been able to cash his check. She hadn't told her mother of the change in ownership, so Jeanne assumed the painting was going to Sylvia. Andrea didn't correct that impression. She found it impossible to speak of Breck to anyone, and to try to explain Breck's determination to have the picture was beyond her powers. She didn't really understand it herself.

On Thursday she left the painting at the framers, after extracting a promise from Kevin that he would notify Breck's office of the whereabouts of the painting. Kevin would charge her account once Breck had chosen the frame. She and Kevin together made several tentative choices and he laid the lengths aside to show Breck when he came. She could tell that Kevin was more than a little curious about this odd way of delivering a painting to a client, but he asked no questions. It was just as well. He would have gotten no answers.

She went back to her apartment for lunch, what she ate of it. While she ate, she scanned the day's delivery of mail. Bills, inquiries, junk mail, she sifted through it all and tossed it glumly on the table. She hadn't really expected anything else, but that little hope that does not die always burgeoned unbidden, determined though she was to quash it. She knew it was foolish. If he had anything to say to her, he wouldn't write. Breck was not a man to tamely write a letter. He'd phone or suddenly appear at the door.

"Andrea, stop mooning over the man like an adolescent! He wanted one thing from you and when he couldn't get it, he had no more use for you." The words echoed into silence in the apartment. Now she was reduced to talking aloud to herself. She'd given herself this lecture so many times the past few days, the tape should be wearing thin. Someday she'd even start believing it.

When she entered her mother's room that afternoon, she should have known. There was a pallid sparkle long absent in her mother's eye, and had she not been so glad to find that this was to be one of Jeanne's increasingly rare "good" days, Andrea would have reached the correct conclusion sooner. As it was, her mother's words were her first intimation of what was to happen.

"Andrea, dear." Her mother's unwontedly firm tone caught her attention at once. It had heavy overtones of "I know you're not going to like this but I want you to do it anyway." When she was a child, it usually presaged a visit to the dentist or to the doctor for routine inoculations. She watched her mother warily.

Jeanne, having caught her daughter's complete attention, waded in at the deep end. "Your father is coming by this afternoon, Andrea. I want you to stay during the visit."

"Mother!" She just couldn't let this pass without objection.

"Andrea, I want to see my husband and my daughter in the same room at the same time once more before I die. I know your feelings and you know mine. I also know what I'm asking of you, but I want you to do it." She reached weakly for Andrea's hand, and Andrea immediately responded, grasping the thin hand firmly. "Please, my dear. You gratify my every whim, and . . ." she continued with a ghost of a smile, "even those I don't know I have. Gratify this one for me too."

There was nothing Andrea could say.

When Devlin entered the room, bearing an ostentatious bouquet of long-stemmed red roses, Andrea thought she would choke on her own bile. The venomous look she shot at him, which her mother couldn't see, left him in no doubt whatsoever that she was here under duress. A red flush stained the back of his neck. Anger or mortification?

While he greeted his wife, Andrea watched the man who was her sire. He was tall and elegantly slim. She owed her own fine-boned elegance and coloring to his genes. He had a facile charm and ready wit, but to Andrea's critical eyes it was the shiny glitter of a mirror, giving him an illusive depth that had no reality. He was a taker and a user, selfish to the marrow, but it was not the innocent selfish egotism of a child. He was an adult egoist, interested in other people only as they related to himself. He took some twisted pleasure from the love Jeanne had steadfastly given him, and God knows he had given *her* cause to hate him. His betrayals littered their lives.

Andrea acknowledged her own share of guilt. In spite of her mother's words, had it not been for the presence of a child, might not Jeanne have left him finally and built herself a better life? Guilt and gratitude. Chains of love forged daily, and ones she'd gladly wear until death snapped the links.

So, she was present during the visit. She did not speak or look directly at her father. She had not looked directly at him since that first black glare when he entered, because now her mother watched the two of them constantly. She would not give her mother additional distress by showing her contempt with such blatant bluntness.

Andrea listened when he spoke to Jeanne, but never commented. Devlin was too canny to risk the snub direct. He knew even Jeanne's presence would not deter Andrea from rebuffing savagely any overtures he might foolishly make. His daughter despised him totally. She was the canker on his nearly nonexistent conscience, and when those clear gray eyes, like his own in color and shape but having a depth his own could never achieve, turned their incisive clarity on him, he always felt something within him blacken and shrivel.

"Devlin, you're looking tired." Jeanne's thin voice evinced concern. "Are you feeling well, dear?"

What grotesque reversal! Andrea writhed inside. She wasn't going to be able to take much more of this. If her father didn't leave soon, she would have to, against her mother's wishes or not. It would be better to go than be actively sick to her stomach. Even now the light lunch she had managed to choke down was assuming the proportions of a large lead ball somewhere near her solar plexus.

Andrea ground her teeth silently as Devlin reacted to his wife's concern for his well-being.

"It's that damned Breck Carson!" Andrea's head snapped up, but fortunately Devlin's attention was on his wife and he missed her involuntary reaction.

"Breck Carson? The new owner of the company? What's he done, Devlin?" Jeanne was curious.

Please don't let her mention that I've gone out with him, Andrea prayed silently. Her father was bound to hear, sooner or later, through the grapevine, but let it be later. She didn't think she could control herself if he gibed at her in front of her mother.

"He's got the whole company bustling like an ant-hill that's been stirred with a stick. He's in New York on business, but while he's gone, he has the auditors ripping the books to pieces. I think he plans to take the place apart completely and put it back together a different way . . . a top-to-bottom reorganization, in fact."

"How tiring for you, Devlin. I suppose you have to supervise it all while he's away. But a reorganization won't affect you, will it, dear?" Jeanne voiced the soothing concern that had always made her so valuable to his ego.

"Well, actually, I don't have anything to do with the upheaval directly," Devlin responded to Jeanne's question. "Carson has his own management team. He works with them to decide what exactly is to be done, but he usually doesn't turn them loose quite so soon or with such fervor. He's actually in New York to complete the final transfer. His people did a preliminary work-up on the company when negotiations began, and we knew there'd be some changes made, but it's most unusual to start this kind of operation before the final papers are even signed."

Andrea listened intently. Her father was worried about something, all right. She had caught faint traces the night of the company party, but the worry was now more distinct, more personal. Of course, her father always took everything personally. She fired a blind shot.

"It almost sounds as though Mr. Carson is looking for something, doesn't it?" she drawled. "Auditors at the books give rise to such unsavory and disquieting speculations. Perhaps someone's been cooking the accounts," she said to the room at large. She couldn't bring herself to address her father, even to set a sarcastic barb.

Narrow-eyed, she watched him pale and then flush dark red. Somehow she'd struck home! Things must really be happening at the company if the odor of malfeasance was wafting through the rarefied executive air. If there was a scandal, executive vice-presidential heads might roll, although she'd have presumed her father more than adept at survival techniques. He had the fine art of throwing a fellow passenger to any wolves gaining on the troika down pat. He'd even been known to brag about some particularly slick example of backstabbing in the privacy of his own home.

She considered the personal implications. Doing some lightning-fast calculations, she reassured herself that she'd be able to assume full responsibility for her mother's medical bills, should the need arise. It would mean working flat out, but the work would be good for her and it wouldn't give her time to think. She'd almost welcome the chance.

But, she shrugged mentally, it'd probably not come to that. Even if there was something rotten traced back to a man under her father's jurisdiction, she was sure he'd have a scapegoat ready to stuff down the wolves' throats, allowing Devlin Thomas to walk away without a tooth mark on him.

Her father left soon after, mouthing promises to come again in a few days. Andrea vowed *she* wouldn't be present the next time, whatever form of moral blackmail her mother brought to bear.

The rest of the week passed slowly. The forced meeting with her father was a darker spot in a uniformly black week. Even the weather was against her. When her car had a flat tire in the middle of a driving rainstorm, Andrea was contemplating shaking her fist at the heavens when a very gallant man stopped and changed the tire for her. He also asked her for a date, and she told him she was engaged to be married. He was very nice about it, if a trifle wistful. She felt rather guilty about deceiving him, but not guilty enough to accept a date with him. He'd probably turn out to be Jack the Nine-handed Wonder.

She still slept poorly, although her appetite had improved marginally. Johnny called several times, but she put him off, the first time because her mother was sinking so badly. The second time he called she told him she was swamped with catch-up work, now that her mother had improved.

She was behind, but it was mainly because she had developed a distressing tendency to sit and stare at blank pieces of paper instead of filling them with the required artwork. She told herself that if it wasn't so pathetic, it'd be funny. She was behaving like a Victorian miss pining away for love. Pep talks didn't do much good either!

CHAPTER FOUR

She was staring moodily out of the window, watching the rain sheet by. It was almost midmorning, but outside there was the crepuscular half-light of early evening. She had been up since six and had at last managed to get fairly deeply into the most urgent assignment. Yesterday, Saturday, she had received a query from the patient art director whose firm had sent her the commission. There had been several "I know you're busy, but . . ." phrases and, grimly determined, she had set her clock for the early hour the night before.

She had broken for coffee twenty minutes ago and the last of it was now cold and unappealing in the bottom of her cup. Her fingers were smudged and stained and her jeans and T-shirt were liberally spotted with acrylic paint. She had been trying out a spatter effect and it had worked.

In her preoccupation she hadn't consciously noted the elevator sounds, or maybe he just came up the stairs, but the sudden double knock startled her so much that she knocked her cup off the window ledge. She caught it before it shattered on the floor, and fortunately there wasn't more than a quarter cup of cold coffee left. Unfortunately, like blood, a little coffee goes a long way and she added coffee stains to the paint and ink adorning her clothes.

She looked over at the door, waiting for the knock to come again. Maybe she was having auditory hallucinations. The double knock resounded through the living room again, this time accompanied by a full-throated, "Andrea, open the door!"

"All right, all right, I'm coming," she yelled as she balanced the now empty cup back on the windowsill. Holding her wet T-shirt away from her midriff, she went hastily to the door and released the dead bolt.

When he heard the lock release, Breck didn't wait for Andrea to turn the doorknob. He thrust the door open, forcing her to leap agilely out of the way.

"What took you so long?" he growled. He looked at her closely. "You look terrible. You must have lost ten pounds, and you couldn't afford them."

"I spilled my coffee, and it was only five," she snapped back defensively, already badly off-balance. "I'm going to change my shirt. You can mop up the mess over by the window. It was your fault I spilled it."

"Was it hot? Did you burn yourself?" He grabbed her arm, and she wrenched it away. "Let me see, Andrea."

She backed away. "No, it wasn't hot, Breck. It was just the dregs of the cup I had while taking a break. I'm just wet," she finished as she turned and fled. When she shut the bedroom door behind her, she was breathing as though *she* had sprinted up the six flights of stairs.

He was really, really here. Big, blond, flesh and blood, and what did he want? She was excited and apprehensive at the same time. Her head told her to be wary, but her heart, which had cost her five

93

pounds and a lot of lost sleep, could only race uncontrollably.

She changed into dry clothes as quickly as her shaky fingers would allow. He might just decide to follow her into the bedroom if he thought she was taking too long, and she had to avoid that at all costs. He had come back, but she didn't know why and until she did, she wasn't going to take any chances.

When she came out of the bedroom, she heard kitchen sounds and deduced that he had taken her literally and was cleaning up the spilled coffee. She hadn't really meant for him to do it. It had just been something to say on the spur of the moment. But, if he was occupied for the moment, perhaps she could scrub a bit of the paint and ink off her hands . . . and face, she added when she saw herself in the bathroom mirror.

She scrubbed away most of the spots and daubs, but she couldn't do much about the dark shadows beneath her eyes or the drawn hollows in her cheeks, which accentuated her cheekbones. She had to admit that she was just this side of being interestingly gaunt. Another three or four pounds and she'd have made it. From his comments at his first sight of her, Breck didn't approve, and would probably tell her so in greater detail as soon as she went back into the living room. It wouldn't do to let him think *he* had been the cause of a decline!

She dusted on a little blusher and rubbed on some lipstick, tucked in her shirt, and left the sanctuary of the bathroom.

Breck had cleaned up the spattered coffee and had the water boiling for more.

"Is all you have instant?" He indicated the jar of crystals disdainfully.

"Yes. I always put so much sugar and milk in it that it doesn't seem worth going the gourmet, grind-your-own-beans route. I drink it because it's hot and for the caffeine, not the taste. Instant coffee was invented for philistines like me." She nearly laughed out loud at the appalled expression that flitted across his face. "I gather you're a coffee snob. Just add an extra dollop of milk and another spoonful of sugar and you'll never know the difference," she advised him cheekily as she busied herself with clean cups and saucers.

He muttered something sotto voce and took the shrilly whistling kettle off the burner, setting it on a cool coil, while she spooned the dry coffee into the cups. He stirred his own with some violence, not taking her advice to add sugar and milk. She almost expected him to clutch his throat and cry, "Arrgh," after his first sip, but his control was equal to greater tests than her coffee.

He waited politely for her to precede him into the living room and when she sat down on the couch, close to one end, he sat down in the center and, considering his bulk, uncomfortably close. She sipped at her coffee nervously and tried to breathe normally. She could tell he was inspecting every shadow and hollow on her face and it wouldn't have surprised her if he had grabbed her wrist to take her pulse too.

As she had surmised, he pursued the subject of her appearance, which evidently displeased him greatly. "You look like hell. Been missing me?" This last was said with such pleased arrogance that Andrea was furious.

"No!" she snarled. "My mother was critically ill this past week and I've been by her side. Don't flatter yourself, Breck. I survived your absence very well, as I'm sure you did mine."

She hadn't meant to slash at him so viciously, and she regretted it the moment the words left her lips. Her hand went involuntarily to cover her mouth, as if to hold back more hurtful phrases, but it was too late to recall those already uttered. The grim set of his face told her she'd pay for those biting words, and her eyes were wide and apprehensive as she watched him.

"How is your mother now?" he asked stiffly.

"She's—she's better. She loses ground each time, but she's stable for the moment. The doctor had to increase her dosages again and that affects her heart adversely. It's a vicious cycle. The pain weakens her and the increased medication to ease the pain weakens her too."

Andrea sighed and pushed the hair back from her forehead tiredly. "It's really just a matter of time. Day after agonizing day she lies there, getting frailer and—" Her hands clenched spasmodically in her lap, but he didn't cover them or offer any comfort. "She was a lovely woman once. My father isn't attracted to any other kind."

She'd given him the opening he was waiting for. His face grew grimmer and sterner, and Andrea stiffened. He looked . . . savage, and then he smiled. The smile made her shudder. Suddenly she was terrified and she started up from the couch. She didn't get more than halfway up before he wrenched her back down beside him with a cruel grip on her forearm.

"Don't run away, Andrea," he said with silky menace.

"You're hurting my arm," she gasped. He eased his grip fractionally but didn't release her totally. His blue eyes were blazing at her, and she knew that she was about to pay for her injudicious taunt of moments earlier.

He smoothed the reddened skin of her forearm and his touch was oddly gentle, but his words were at variance with that light caress. "I am sorry, Andrea. I don't want to bruise this soft skin of yours. I now have a proprietary interest in keeping it unblemished."

"And just what is that supposed to mean?" She strove to keep her voice steady, but it quavered slightly. The triumph in his eyes was inexplicable. Surely he didn't mean to *rape* her? But his eyes were running over her as though he owned every inch of her, and her throat went dry. "Breck?"

His hand went out to cup itself around her throat, stroking gently up and down while she watched his face like a mesmerized rabbit. When it slid lower to press down in the vee of her shirt, exerting pressure until the button pulled out of the button hole, she drew in a shaky breath but stayed cautiously still. He was dangerous . . . she sensed it.

His fingers slid lower again, splaying out over the mounded swell of her breasts, his wrist resting against the second button, which was straining from the pressure. His little finger and his thumb spanned from nipple to nipple beneath her bra.

Andrea knew he felt the panicking thud of her heart. It throbbed beneath his warm, hard palm. "Breck?" she questioned him again, quietly, sensing that he was controlled by gossamer-thin threads and afraid to do anything to shatter those fragile strands.

He sighed heavily and slowly lifted his hand away, trailing his fingers across her skin to prolong his contact with her silken soft warmth. Now she noticed the etched lines of weariness that bracketed his mouth and saw that he too had shadows laid beneath his eyes. But where hers gave her an air of fragility, his merely made him look hard and dangerous.

The moment of incipient violence seemed to have passed, but she knew she must tread very warily indeed. Something was wrong, catastrophically wrong, and with a sinking heart she knew it was somehow connected with her father. Breck's face had changed when she mentioned Devlin in passing. He had become . . . triumphant.

"Breck," she said for a third time. "Please. Tell me what it is. What's happened?"

"Your father is a thief," he stated brutally. Her eyes rounded in shock and he smiled again, that mirthless, merciless smile that had so terrified her before.

"I don't understand," she whispered.

"It's very simple, Andrea, darling. We knew there was an embezzler in the company, in a position of trust, before we bought it. My team turned up traces during the preliminary investigation of the books before I closed the deal. The amounts are substantial and have been taken over a period of time, approximately three years, in fact."

He watched her face go bloodlessly white with almost clinical interest. Her eyes shut and her throat muscles rippled as she swallowed. When her eyes opened again, he continued.

"As I say, the amounts are substantial. Not enough to cripple the company, but it would have, should the drain have continued. We didn't know who it was, because it was necessary to do some rather concentrated digging to trace the thefts home to roost, and I wasn't prepared to do that until the company was mine."

Andrea remembered sickly her father's phrase about Breck's auditors "ripping the books apart" and his reaction to her gibe. He hadn't been tired. He had been in a flat panic! An embezzler escapes detection only as long as there is no suspicion. Once scented, all the paper twists and turns are futile. He leaves his track like dirty paw prints through the numbers, and all the auditor has to do is follow the trail back to his lair.

Lecher and thief. What a heritage! She felt fouled, ashamed to meet Breck's eyes. No wonder he had looked at her so oddly. The sins of the fathers . . . If he only knew the rest of it, he wouldn't stand to be in the same room with her.

She kept her head down, looking at her fingers, which were twisting and twining together with an independent life of their own. "Has he been arrested yet?" It was the conventional thing to ask, so she did, though she had no real interest in the answer. She should have, as Breck's next words made clear to her.

"Not yet, darling. That's why I'm here. His fate rests entirely in your hands." He was astounded when she began to laugh.

"Throw him in jail and drop the key in the ocean! Let him pay for his actions for once in his selfish, amoral life." There had been a touch of hysteria in her laugh, but the face she lifted to his was judicially calm. "I'll beg no mercy for him, Breck! He deserves none. Give him to the law." She might have been a Roman matron saying, "Give him to the lions." The tone was implacable, the gesture thumbs-down.

The woman was astounding. Tender and infinitely

loving with her mother, she was capable of an intensity of hatred he had not understood nor plumbed the depths of until now. For a moment he hesitated. Perhaps this was not the way. If she came to hate him as deeply as she did her father, what would it cost him? But it was too late. He realized that now. The mold was set, the die thrown, and he must go on as he began. None of these thoughts broke through his warrior's mask and he nodded slightly.

"As you will, but have you considered the effect on your mother when your father is arrested? She still loves him, I believe?" His tone was calm, merely pointing out an interesting fact.

Andrea went sheet-white. Her mother! How could she have forgotten? In her selfish, *blind* satisfaction, she had forgotten the effect her father's arrest and disgrace would have on her mother. Her thoughts scurried frantically. Maybe they could keep it from her. The nurses would help, as would the doctor. A convenient illness on her father's part, occasional deliveries of flowers in his name. Surely they could manage it for the short time still left to her.

Every one of these thoughts showed on her expressive face, and Breck was watching her intently. He relaxed slightly. It was going to be all right. Her reaction to her father's probable fate had shaken him, knocking his house of dream cards askew.

"It won't work, Andrea," he said gently.

"What?" she said abstractedly, still deep in plans. "What won't work?"

"You won't be able to keep it from your mother. If your father is arrested, she'll find out." His tone was still gentle. He could afford to be gentle now.

"No, she won't," Andrea said decisively. "It won't be easy, but the nurses and doctors will help. We'll censor the newspapers. I generally read them to her anyway. She'll be told he has a cold and can't visit, and I'll send her flowers and messages in his name. She . . . she hasn't long," her voice broke on the words, "and I can keep it from her. I have to. She's borne enough for his sake."

"You won't be able to keep it from her," he repeated with gentle persistence. "She'll find out."

"How?" snapped Andrea. "I've just told you—"

"Because I'll make sure she does, Andrea," he promised her.

She couldn't believe her ears, but one look at his face told her he meant what he had just said. And he could do it, she knew with a sinking heart. Anyone ruthless enough could get through the lax security of the nursing home. They could guard against accidental enlightenment, but not against someone determined to bring the news to her mother.

"Why, Breck? Why?" It was a cry from the heart. "Do you hate me so much?"

"Hate you, Andrea, darling?" His voice was silkily smooth again. "On the contrary. I don't hate you at all. I want you rather desperately, in fact."

She could only stare at him uncomprehendingly. He continued, his voice deepening savagely. "You've tormented my dreams and tortured my days. I hear your voice in other women's voices. The scent of your hair teases my senses . . . a memory I can't expunge. You haunt me, coming between me and my work and my pleasures, and so I'm going to exorcise you. I'm going to take you, to satiate myself with you until I no longer want you. Since you won't come to me freely, you'll come to me under duress, but come to me you will."

"You're insane," she whispered.

101

"Perhaps." He shrugged, and then his lips quirked, but there was no mirth in those blue eyes, which raked her face. "Just like the song says, 'Mad about the girl.'"

She scanned his face thoroughly. He had to be joking or bluffing or . . . He wasn't. She was defeated and she knew it.

"All right, Breck. You win. Spell out your terms." Her voice was passionless and level, reflecting her sudden numb acceptance of the unbelievable.

"You'll come to me?" he insisted.

"Yes."

"All right. I won't prosecute your father. He'll be forcibly retired, but no criminal charges will be filed. In spite of all precautions, slipups do occur, and if he was charged, your mother might hear of it. Besides, it wouldn't look right if I prosecuted my father-in-law."

Andrea's head jerked up. "Father-in-law?" she repeated.

"Of course. You weren't interested in any other arrangement. You've won, Andrea. You'll get a ring and all the legal benefits, and I'll get . . . you. I'm paying a high price for you, my freedom and over one hundred thousand dollars. That's approximately how much your father stole. See that you're worth it."

Her face seemed to hollow and tauten, the clean, firm bone structure showing with precision beneath the suddenly pale cheeks. "This marriage. It's nothing more to you than a legalized affair? A necessity because of my moral scruples against climbing into bed with anyone other than a legal husband?"

He shrugged. "You made the terms clear last week, Andrea. I'm prepared to abide by them."

"And if I will not marry you?"

"I will prosecute your father to the fullest extent of the law and make sure your mother knows about it." She could discern no emotion in his voice or face. He was simply stating facts.

"Even though you know what it will mean, would do, to her?"

He met her eyes firmly. "Yes. I want you."

Her eyes closed briefly and when they opened, they were a flat, dull gray, all light quenched. "You win, Breck. I hope your victory turns to ashes in your mouth, but you win this round."

He relaxed back on the couch. There was no triumph in his eyes. They were hooded and guarded. "We'll be married this Wednesday. I'll make all the arrangements."

A smile that bared her teeth stopped the rest of his sentence. "Oh, no, Breck. I won't *marry* you. When I marry, if I ever marry, it will be to a man I can love and respect. You see, I still believe in marriage, as an institution, in spite of the none too cheery examples I've seen. If I marry, I plan to marry for life. When I make my vows, I'll mean them and do my best to keep them."

He made an involuntary motion that she quelled with a lift of her hand. "I said you've won," she assured him. "I'll come to you. I'll be your mistress, but I won't be your wife. Until my mother dies, I'll be your mistress. When she can't be hurt anymore, you can prosecute my father and leave him to rot for all of me." Her words fell stony cold on his ears, beating against his skin like so many icy pellets of sleet.

Now her eyes blazed, burning bright and hating hot. "You'll have the use of my body, Breck, until my mother is dead, but that's all you'll have of me. Not one word of tenderness, not one ounce of compassion or concern. If you're tired, if you're hurt, if you're sick, plan to go elsewhere for succor, because you won't find it with me! Those are *my* terms, Breck, and they're the only terms you'll get from me."

"And what will your mother say? Won't such an arrangement upset her?"

"My mother won't know. You'll see to it. If she finds out, our *bargain*"—the sneer was perceptible—"is at an end. She's insulated from the world, sedated because of the steadily increasing pain, and my father and I are her only visitors. You'll make sure he realizes it's in his interest to keep quiet about our arrangement."

He capitulated. "As you will, Andrea. I'll arrange to have your things moved to my apartment. You can keep this place as a studio, until I can arrange to have one set up for you at my apartment. Once you have finished whatever commercial assignments you're still obligated to do, you can begin to paint seriously full-time."

He got up and began to pace. "Do you pay your mother's medical bills? I'll take over those, so you won't need your commercial commissions, and I'll take over the rent on this apartment as well. Give me the name of your bank and I'll arrange to have a monthly allowance paid into your checking account."

Andrea was off the couch in a flash and confronting him angrily. "You didn't listen to me, Breck. I'm to be your mistress, not your wife. My studio and apartment stay as they are. I won't live in your apartment with you. You can visit me, but I support my-

104

self and I'll take nothing from you . . . no presents, no furs or jewels or whatever are the perks of a mistress. Our bargain has only two factors: you promise not to prosecute my father while my mother lives, and for that promise I will pay you with my body."

He flinched and she laughed bitterly. "Too crude, Breck? How shall I dress it up? What words would you like for me to use to describe our forthcoming relationship?"

His fists clenched. "You've got a shrewish-sharp tongue, my girl," he said through gritted teeth.

"It must be the company I keep," she threw back at him.

"Give me a key to this apartment," he ordered her.

She turned away and walked over to the kitchen, where she rummaged in a small drawer. She pulled out a metal ring with several keys attached to it and took one off, returning the others to the drawer. She walked back to confront him, and the hand that held the key out to him trembled slightly.

He grasped the key, hand and all, and jerked her into his arms. His kiss was hungry, punitive, and bruising. She didn't struggle, but neither did she respond. When he let her go, she swayed slightly and raised her hand to feel her puffy lips.

"I have another engagement tonight," he informed her. Her eyes flew up to his face, their expression unreadable. "A working dinner with my bankers," he continued smoothly. "I won't see you until tomorrow, probably late in the afternoon. We'll go out to dinner, unless you prefer to cook a meal for me." His voice was mocking.

She glared at him.

"No? Ah, yes, that must come under the heading

of wifely duties, which you are not obligated to perform. Pity. Your father said you're an excellent cook."

"I go to visit my mother every afternoon, Breck," she warned him. "I'll continue to do so."

"Of course," he agreed. He dropped another kiss, lighter this time, on her lips. "Until tomorrow, my darling."

He shut the door behind him softly, then winced as it shook and the sound of shattering glass and splashing liquid came clearly through the panels. He shook his head and moved off down the hall, thinking, I hope she gets the coffee stains out of the rug.

Andrea stood looking at the dripping door, her whole body shaking. This couldn't be happening to her. It must be a nightmare that she'd wake from in a moment. She couldn't have just promised to become Breck Carson's *mistress!*

She bent mechanically to pick up the shattered pieces of the cup she had hurled at the door. A sharp-edged splinter pricked her finger and she sucked the little welling drop of red. It was true. Real blood.

More carefully she picked up the bits of cup and then got a dishtowel to mop up the brown splotches of coffee. She moved as though she were suddenly an old woman, stiff and jerky and incredibly ancient. Oh, Breck, her mind cried. How could you do this to me, to both of us? We should have come together in love and tenderness and trust, not lust and disillusion.

"I can't do it." She spoke the words aloud, flinging them into the air of the empty apartment. "I won't! I won't be like my mother!" It was the ultimate irony, and the tears began to stream down her face

106

as she thought back to the days immediately after Jeanne's accident.

She knew her father had been seeing still another woman, but he had been more blatant than usual and he and her mother had quarreled. In a frenzy of humiliation and despair, Jeanne had driven off in the car, to be brought, broken and crushed, from the shredded ruins of her car several hours later. The police had said it was an unavoidable accident, not her mother's fault. A diesel hauler, with an inexperienced driver at the wheel, had jackknifed when he applied the brakes too swiftly, trying to avoid a car that cut in front of him. Jeanne had been caught in the resultant accident.

No, not her fault. Andrea knew why she had been out on the road that day. She knew whose fault it was and she told him, her young face twisted in rage and hurt. She had often heard her mother cry pillow-muffled tears in the night when her father had "worked late," and she had seen her mother's face when a jeweler's bill for a bracelet and earring set she had never received came to the house by mistake.

And then, stung by guilt and the ruthless mirror of truth his daughter held before his face, Devlin Thomas did the unforgivable. He told her the truth of her birth. Perhaps in some twisted way he meant to drive a wedge between the woman he called wife and the daughter he had sired, but instead it finished him completely and forever in his daughter's eyes. Where she had despised, now she hated. She had packed her belongings and left his house that night.

Jeanne was not her blood mother. Devlin had sired her on one of his mistresses, and when the girl, for she had been little more than that, had died in child-

107

birth, he had brought the child to Jeanne. They had no children of their own.

Jeanne had named her and loved her and had never by word or deed ever been anything but a true and loving mother. Devlin had used them both. Jeanne to care for his chance sired child—he had admitted that he had tried to get the girl to abort the unwanted baby but she refused—Andrea to tie Jeanne more tightly to him, had it been necessary. Jeanne loved the child and would do nothing to break the rapport between them. Devlin did not say it, but Andrea knew him well: knew he would have held the threat of revealing her parentage over Jeanne by implication if nothing else.

Daughter of a lecher, child of a whore. Soon to be concubine to a man she had been close to loving. Had she only herself to consider, she might well have slashed her wrists and been done with the pain of living. Instead she wept, bitter, hopeless tears and deep, racking sobs. She lay on the living room rug, curled in an embryonic ball, and cried until her tears were burned dry and she could breathe only in great gulping gasps of air that seared her lungs.

When the sobbing abated, she climbed shakily to her feet and wove her way into the bathroom to hang limply over the toilet while her abused nervous system took its revenge. She retched until nothing was left, splashed water on her face, and went to the phone. With shaking fingers she dialed the number of the nursing home, identified herself to the nurse who answered, and said, "Tell my mother that I'll come to see her this evening. I won't be able to come this afternoon, but I will stop by soon after supper." She listened for a moment and then said, "No, nothing's wrong. I've just had a bit of car trouble and it won't be fixed until late this afternoon. Please don't let her worry. I'll be there tonight without fail."

Andrea knew the nurse didn't believe her. She couldn't make her voice sound normal, but the nurse wouldn't alarm Jeanne. She'd make the excuse believable. It was the first time Andrea had ever missed an afternoon visit, but she had no choice at all. She couldn't see Jeanne while she was in this state. Another debt laid to her father's and Breck's accounts.

After she hung up, Andrea went into her bedroom and drew the drapes at the window. The darkness was a haven, a cave to hide in, a place of short oblivion. She undressed in the dark and climbed into bed, pulling the covers up over her head in a temporary retreat from a reality she found unbearably painful.

When she woke, she was resigned. It was all very well to cry, "I will not!" to the empty air, but it didn't change the situation. The mermaid was hooked and gaffed and the first searing rasps of air were excruciating.

Andrea knew what she had to face. Disillusionment. An unwilling attraction to a man who was arrogant and callous and ready to use her for the gratification of his desires, as her father had used her real mother.

"He would have married you," a little voice whispered mockingly.

"But only because he thought he couldn't have me any other way," she rejoined with bitter realization. "If coming to him in lust will be degradation and shame, what hell would a marriage founded on such a basis be? What sadistically refined torture!"

And with these spoken words, she made her plans. She knew the worst now. She was no longer torn apart between her head and her heart, divided by hope and wishes. Breck was inescapable while her mother lived, but when she died, the mermaid would rip herself from the hook. Though it ripped out her heart as well, she would swim away into the untraceable depths, and no bait would tempt her up toward the sun again.

The visit to her mother went better than Andrea had expected. Jeanne seemed to accept her tale of a fairly minor mechanical defect with equanimity, although Andrea wasn't sure how much was due to her histrionic ability and how much was due to the increased dosages of painkiller. Jeanne was slipping away from life steadily now, making no effort to delay her going. Andrea knew her time could be measured in weeks only, and very few at that.

The next morning Andrea rose very early. She had an incentive to work now and she intended to finish as many commissions as was humanly possible before her mother's death. She would need as much cash as she could gather together, readily available, at least enough to carry her for a while until she was earning again. When she knew the end was near, she would notify her clients to hold their assignments until she sent her new address. She would also caution them not to reveal her whereabouts to *anyone* without her specific permission.

Her initial lease on the apartment had run out and her month-to-month rental would prove no barrier when the time came for her to leave. Her furniture could go into storage. It was good, but there were no sentimental attachments. Someday, if she wished, she could send for it. Anything else, her pictures and clothes, would go with her in the car. Her rather spartan life-style the past few years hadn't left her many personal possessions, and what there was, was portable.

She worked swiftly and with intense concentration, something she hadn't been able to do for far too long, it seemed. The work she had started yesterday was done before her morning break. She'd mail it and a short cover letter to go with it on her way to the nursing home this afternoon.

She dived back into her work. While she was busy she didn't have to think about the evening . . . and Breck. Anytime her thoughts strayed to him, she got a queasy sensation in the pit of her stomach. She was inexperienced but not ignorant. Modern school theories being what they were, she had a complete, clinical grounding in the biological functions of the human body . . . all of them. But the translation of theory into practice was another thing altogether.

In spite of, or because of her background, she had hung on tenaciously to the dream of the one man, the antithesis of her father's type, who would cherish and value her as a woman and a person and to whom she would cleave for the rest of her life. Her unwilling attraction to Breck had shaken her preconceived dreams, and the reality of what she was about to do filled her with self-loathing.

To be carried away by the passion of the moment, overwhelmed by inflamed senses, seduced, in fact, would be easier to bear in the long run than this cold-blooded barter of her body. Breck would take her with premeditated passion and what was worse, he might even be able to make her respond, resist him though she would! Ruthlessly honest with herself, she had to admit that, for Breck alone, she felt the stirrings of a woman's curiosity toward a man. Something deep and primitive woke within her when

111

she looked at him, something her fear of her sensual heritage could not quite quell. She didn't *want* to be like her biological parents, a slave to her desires!

She wanted more out of life, a deep relationship that touched on all levels, not just the physical. She hated Breck for being unable or unwilling to give her what she wanted and for perhaps destroying for all time her ability to ever find such a relationship with another man.

So, she would run. When her mother died, she would leave, totally cut loose from her past life and do her best to completely block it from her thoughts. Maybe in time, unhampered by ties of duty and love and hate, she could at last become the woman she wished to be. New places, new faces: they would be her curative. Somewhat comforted by her plans, she worked on.

She ate lunch on the way to the nursing home, succumbing to the indigestible efficiency of a drive-through hamburger chain because she was pressed for time. She still had to pick up her daily knick-knack for Jeanne, and the finding of just what she wanted might take some looking. Jeanne's increasing weakness and dimming vitality made the task of finding something to rouse her interest ever harder, and Andrea finally resorted to a new music cassette of some classical guitar selections by Roderigo and Albéniz. The crisp, intricate fingering was attention riveting and should distract Jeanne for a while at least.

Jeanne was pleased with the new tape and they played it several times during the afternoon. They decided that the young guitarist did not yet have the mature precision of Segovia but that his youthful fire and exuberance made for a stirring performance. Andrea promised to try to obtain more of his tapes, very pleased that her mother was so responsive.

She stayed longer than was her normal practice, both to make up for the shortened visit of the day before and from an unexpressed reluctance to go back to her apartment. She knew when she went home she would again be prey to the fears and antici- pations of what the coming evening would bring. When she went back, she would have to prepare for Breck's arrival and all that that portended.

She parked the car in its accustomed slot and with dragging footsteps entered the elevator. She hadn't the energy to tackle the stairs as she usually did. She slumped against the wall as the elevator creaked and groaned its way upward. Maybe it'd get stuck be- tween floors and she could spend the night, alone, on its hard, gritty floor. She laughed grimly. Breck would probably climb down the cables hand over hand to get to her.

No, there was to be no escape for her. As women had been from time immemorial, she was chained captive for a conquering warrior. Dressed up with flowers as that first invitation had been, if invitation was indeed the proper word, or phrased with all the naked power of the victor as that last ultimatum had been, she had known all along what he wanted, meant to have.

Suddenly a grim smile twisted her mouth. She was remembering the frustrated fury in his voice when he told her, "No man enjoys making love to a rag doll." Perhaps, even if she could not prevent what was to come, she could at least ensure that Breck took no pleasure in her. A limp and passive body beneath his, a body that might belong to "anywoman." With a sure instinct she knew that she could inflict a grievous wound by merely lying unresponsive before his drive to possess. He might say he desired her body, but the shell without the substance of her mind and spirit to fill it would avail him nothing. Could she do it? It was her only defense. She had to try.

She opened the door to her apartment, stepped inside, and froze in shock. A desk she'd never seen, a beautiful, massive walnut rolltop, was shoved against one wall, papers protruding from its cubby holes. A black, businesslike phone and a small dictating unit sat on its paper-littered surface along with a used coffee cup; one of her coffee cups. Beside the couch various components of a stereo system had been arranged and there were record and tape cassette holders next to that.

She heard movement in the kitchen and swung to confront the intruder. Breck came out of the kitchen, a coffee pot in hand. It was not her coffee pot. She didn't own one.

He really doesn't like instant coffee, flitted insanely through her mind.

He walked calmly over to the desk and poured himself another cup of coffee. Then he lifted the pot inquiringly in her direction, eyebrow quirked.

"How was your mother this afternoon, Andrea?" he asked politely. When she didn't answer immediately, he continued, "You look tired. It's just as well I've decided we'll eat in tonight."

She could only gape at him. Her eye was caught by several cartons of books and a partially assembled bookshelf. He noticed her glance and explained, "I didn't get around to putting the shelves together. There were several phone calls and some things that had to be taken care of right away. I'll do them tomorrow and then we can get rid of the cartons.

114

Your bookshelves didn't have enough room for my books too."

"You can't—" Her voice failed. She licked her lips and tried again. "You can't just move that stuff in here. This is my apartment. You have no right to—to —"

"To live here with you?" he finished for her. His grin was devilish. "Well, since you won't live with me, I will live with you. Luckily your bedroom is large and there is plenty of room for the king-size bed I had delivered and the extra chest of drawers. That chaste single bed has been sent to the Salvation Army. Since we won't be having guests, we don't need a guest bed. I put the extra linen in that cupboard in the bathroom, but we'll have to get a spread for the bed later. I doubt if we'll be able to match the fabric of the drapes, but it should be fairly easy to coordinate some solid color for the time being. I also got us some new towels. I like big thick ones, and yours all seem to be small and fairly threadbare."

"I must be going insane," she whispered. Then her voice strengthened and she hissed, "Get out, Breck. Get out of my apartment!"

He put the pot down carefully on a stack of papers and folded his arms negligently, leaning one hip against the side of the desk. "Just what did you envision, Andrea?" he drawled mockingly. "That I would visit you once or twice a week, stay an hour or so, and depart?"

"I tried not to think about you at all," she snapped.

He laughed, enjoying her helpless, seething, *impotent* fury. "Oh, no, my darling mistress-to-be." He seemed to savor the words. "I want more of you than that. I intend to have much more of you than that.

While you're mine, you'll be all mine. Whenever I want you, I'll take you."

His face hardened and his lips thinned into a cruel line. "You'll see no other men while you're my woman, and that includes John McKay I'll be here to make sure of that, although I think McKay got the message," he informed her with unmistakable implication.

"What have you done? What did you tell Johnny?" Her voice was a croak. This was unbelievable.

"He called a little while ago, to ask you out, presumably. He seemed surprised when I answered the phone. Thought he had the wrong number, in fact." Breck chuckled slightly. "Of course, he didn't recognize my voice, but I assured him that he did indeed have the right number. He identified himself and I did the same. I also told him I lived here now too and I'd be glad to give you any messages when you got back from visiting your mother at the nursing home. There was no message," Breck finished with savage satisfaction.

Andrea could have scratched his eyes out. She'd never be able to face Johnny again. "You promised that no one would know. You lied to me!" Furious tears burned in her eyes and her hands arched into claws. She sprang at him, out of control, intending to do as much damage to him as she possibly could. At that moment she hated him with a hatred she had reserved only for her father.

He sidestepped her rush easily, pivoting to one side with catlike agility. He encircled her with steel-hard arms, imprisoning her outstretched arms by her sides with easy strength. She kicked and struggled until she was breathless with rage, but he held her

116

without hurting her in any way, merely confining her to keep her from hurting either of them.

When she had calmed slightly, he said quietly, "I didn't break my promise, Andrea. I only agreed that your mother would not know. All of this could have been avoided, you know. I would have married you. I will still marry you. I have no desire to humiliate you, but I will not connive to keep our relationship a secret. I have no plans to sneak into and out of your warm bed, to leave your arms and drive back across town to a cold, empty apartment."

He turned her to face him. There was an odd, guarded look on his face, but she would not lift her eyes to read it. "Andrea, shall we be married after all? You have only to say the word and I'll arrange it still."

Andrea was hot and cold by turns. She didn't really even listen to Breck's words, so deeply affected was she by the knowledge that to the world she had now been proclaimed this man's plaything, his whore. She was her real mother all over again, she thought wildly. What was bred in the bone and blood always came out, struggle how she would to avoid her fate. Now all that was left to her was to hurt this man as badly as he had hurt her.

She leaned back as far as she could in his pinioning arms and looked him squarely in the eyes, her own a flat, bleak gray. "I hate you, Breck Carson. I'll never forgive you for this. I won't marry you! I won't tie myself in any way to a man I despise as much as I despise my father. You've forced me into this situation and now you've branded me before the world, before a man I liked and respected. I might even have wanted to marry him someday," she deliberately inserted to strike out at him.

117

She would never have married Johnny. He had been a friend, not a lover, but Breck was a possessive man and she knew instinctively that to link herself with Johnny was to drive a dirk through a weak chink in his armor. She wanted Breck to writhe as she was writhing and she would use any weapons she had on hand to make him bleed.

She succeeded all too well. His eyes blazed at her and his grip tightened until she could have groaned with the pain. "So you choose to be my mistress rather than my wife—" he began in furious tones.

"I don't *choose* to be your mistress," she interrupted him fiercely, determined to prick him again. "If I had free choice, I'd never set eyes on you again!"

"But you don't have free choice, Andrea," he ground out between clenched teeth. "You have no choice. You've agreed to become my mistress and your choice is made. You have a lot to learn about being a mistress, Andrea, darling." His voice had dropped to a menacing purr and she started to struggle fiercely again, terror in her wildly twisting body.

He swept her up into his arms. She might as well have been caressing him for all the effect she was having against his massive strength. He continued in the same purring tone as he looked down at her, his eyes flaring with triumphant possession, "It will be my pleasure to teach you all you need to know, and your first lesson will begin right now."

CHAPTER FIVE

He strode over to the bedroom door, carrying her easily, and shouldered it open. When it slammed shut behind them, Andrea went rigid in his arms.

The bedroom was dim, shadowed, but not dark. Andrea watched in horrified fascination as Breck strode toward a bed that seemed acres wide. It had been made up with darkly patterned sheets and matching blankets. He swept the top covers back with one hand and then dropped her, gasping, on the bed.

She immediately tried to scramble over to the other side of the bed to get away, but he caught her before she had covered even a quarter of the distance. He pulled her firmly back where he had dropped her and loomed menacingly over her, gigantic in the dim room.

"There's no escape now, Andrea. You'll only hurt yourself if you fight me." His voice was implacable and his hands went to the buttons of his shirt.

This was really happening to her. Her stunned immobility had the quality of some small wild creature petrified by the lights of an onrushing car, hypnotized by its swiftly approaching doom.

"Don't bother looking at me like a doe about to be shot by the hunter, my sweet, desirable mistress," he informed her grimly as he pulled the unbuttoned shirt out of his jeans. "You'll go to your fate willingly. The little death will be most enjoyable, I promise you."

Her eyes were riveted to the masculine perfection of the naked torso exposed beneath the shirt he was removing. His chest was smooth, with plates of strong muscle layered over the rib cage, and the bunched power of his shoulders and biceps as he removed the shirt told her how he had quelled her ineffectual struggles so easily. Small flat nipples broke the smoothness of his skin and a faint line of golden hair ran down from his navel, disappearing into his low-slung jeans.

The artist in her was forced to respond to the sculptured grace of broad, muscled shoulders tapering into narrow waist, but the inexperienced girl felt her throat go dry as his long-fingered hands moved toward the snap and zipper at his waistband. For the moment he merely hooked his thumbs in the belt loops and then his hands were moving again, toward her!

Like a rag doll, she lay passive as he unbuttoned her shirt, pulled it from her unresisting body, and stripped off her bra as well. He ran an exploratory, caressing hand over her breasts before loosening her skirt, removing it and her shoes and tossing them all in a heap on the floor. He finished stripping her, and when she lay naked to his gaze, he stood for a long moment admiring the graceful sweep of her long-legged body against the dark sheets.

"More beautiful than I imagined," he said huskily and began to strip off the rest of his own clothing. He didn't take his eyes off her the whole time. Even when he sat beside her hips to remove his shoes, he stayed half turned toward her, eyes roving restlessly over the length of her.

Even had he turned his back to her, Andrea would not have tried to bolt again. A fatalistic calm had come to her aid and she was blessedly numb, detached from what was happening to her. Later she would hate again, would rage and strike out with wounding words, but now she was not even embarrassed at their mutual nudity. No man had ever seen her thus, and while she had drawn from live models in her art classes, theirs had been a sexless angle and curve of line, not the heated touch of firm skin over sliding muscle and long, hard bone, mingled with the slightly musky scent of aroused male.

Her breathing was even and her pulse seemed to slam through her veins in an achingly slow, deep rhythm. Breck bent to her, lifting her further toward the center of the bed, and slid in next to her. She shivered once, convulsively, at the initial touch of his hands on her body as he moved her over, but made no other sign of awareness.

He grasped her chin in one hand, turning her face toward his, and forced her to meet his eyes. There was a curiously blank blindness in her silver-gray, dark-pupiled stare, as though she looked through and beyond him. He studied her face closely and then smiled mirthlessly.

"You won't escape me that way, my darling Andrea. I'll pull your spirit back from whatever far distance you seek to send it. Your mind is anchored in your beautiful body and here it will stay, stay to share and enjoy what I'm going to do to you now."

He began to caress her lightly, feather-touch strokes that goose-pimpled her skin, sweeping from her shoulders to her hips in delicate patterns, bring-

121

ing to life every sensor in her skin. He watched the pupils of her eyes expand and darken involuntarily.

"I may hurt you a bit this first time, Andrea," he murmured softly, "but I'll pleasure you too, as you will pleasure me."

He did not speak again during that long, slow seduction of the senses, but watched her intently for the betraying signs of quickened breathing and hardening nipples, the little gasps she could not control and the whimper escaping through softly parted lips as he teased and touched them with lips and tongue.

His hands, his mouth tantalized and tormented her, learning every throbbing inch of her, gently, inexorably possessing her before he actually took her. When at last he moved over her, he could no longer see her eyes. They were closed. But her arms went around his neck to pull him to her and her mouth opened beneath his own in a wordless, hungry passion that told him what he wanted to know.

He caught the small pain cry in his mouth, swallowing it, and the subsequent little moans of pleasure as though they were delicious bites of some honeyed fruit. When she came at last to that pinnacle of delight and began her slow slide down to the aftermath of languorous lethargy, he let his own iron control slip free and he too slid down gloriously, after catching a glittering star from the heights of pleasure.

Andrea lay against Breck's chest and listened to his heartbeat beneath her cheek and ear. Her body felt heavy, yet paradoxically featherlight and alive. Later she would hate both Breck and herself, but just now it was too much effort and her weighted eyelids sank down. She slept, slept to wake refreshed as she had not for long months.

Breck pulled the covers over them as the room and

their heated bodies cooled perceptibly, and with Andrea held firmly against his hard length, he slept too. He would wake instantly if she tried to move out of his arms.

When next he woke, they were sleeping spoon fashion and the room was dark, not dim. The temptation to explore the delights his hand was cupping was almost overwhelming, but he regretfully desisted. Andrea was still deeply asleep and the tired pallor of her face when she had come back from her mother's bedside was still etched in his memory. He settled himself more comfortably and waited for her to wake up naturally.

Andrea woke to a cocoon of warmth and pitch black. She started to stretch, cat content, but ran up against an unyielding warm obstruction up and down the length of her back. There was a weight across the side of her rib cage and there was a hand cupped firmly around her breast, the fingers of which were lightly teasing the nipple! She sat up with a stifled scream, and a husky chuckle broke the silence.

"Surely you haven't forgotten me so soon, Andrea, darling?"

She groped blindly for the bedside lamp, but met only the wide expanse of mattress and more mattress. She felt Breck's weight shift on the mattress beside her and with a click, shaded light flooded the room, making their eyes squint as they adjusted after the darkness.

She was sitting up in a huge bed, naked to the waist—and below—in her own bedroom. Breck lay on his back beside her, hands behind his head, regarding her with appreciative eyes and a calm, guarded look on his face. The covers were rumpled around his waist too, but if his naked chest was anything to go by, he was in a like state to herself. Suddenly memory came flooding back and she began to burn with a dark, hot blush.

"Oh, my God!" she moaned and covered her face with her hands, leaning forward into her drawn up knees to rest her forehead. It had really happened. He had made good his promise. He had taken her and she . . . she had *responded!* All memory of the past pleasure was wiped out. All she could think of was that she was now no better than her natural mother. She began to cry, deep, wrenching sobs.

Breck listened for a moment in consternation. This was no maidenly lament for lost virginity. She wept as though her very soul had been reft from her body, heart-deep sobs torn from black anguish. He moved to grasp her shoulders, to pull her back into his arms to try to soothe her. She was tearing herself apart and he had to make her stop.

His touch, his hands on her shoulders made her stop. She rounded on him like a virago. "Damn you to hell, Breck! You've made me no better than my mother. You've made me no better than the promiscuous slut she was." She began to laugh hysterically. "Like father, like daughter. Like mother, like daughter. What's bred in the bone comes out in the blood." It was almost like a chant, and her eyes were silver fires.

There was nothing else he could do. He slapped her sharply across the cheek and she went abruptly silent, her head jerking back and away from the blow. She looked at him unblinkingly, the mark of his hand a red smear of stung skin across her chalkwhite cheek.

"I'm sorry, Andrea," he apologized soothingly. "You were hysterical, and it was the only thing to do to snap you out of it. You didn't know what you were saying. I know you hate your father, but you don't hate your mother, Andrea. You didn't mean what you were saying about her." His voice was gentle, consciously calming. He didn't dare gather her to him, lest she go out of control once more and he didn't think he could bring himself to slap her again.

An indescribably bitter smile spread across her mouth. "I meant every word of it, Breck. And every word was the truth. You thought I was talking about Jeanne, didn't you? That good, brave woman who is mother of my heart but not of my blood." She watched comprehension creep across his face. "You're beginning to understand, aren't you, Breck? Why I refused to have an affair with you until you blackmailed me into it, for Jeanne's sake."

She slid off of the bed and walked over to the closet curtain, moving stiffly but with determination. There was a proud poise about the long line of her spine and she was unselfconscious of her naked glory. She slid back the curtain, idly noting that some of Breck's clothes now hung tidily next to her own. She pulled out a silvery blue velour caftan and slipped it over her head. The room was cool with the evening chill and the smooth warmth of the soft fabric was comfortable.

When she turned back to the bed, Breck was just snapping his jeans at the waist. He hooked his shirt off of the floor and thrust his arms into the sleeves, but didn't button it up. His feet, like her own, were still bare but she didn't wait for him to put his shoes on. She left the room, moving on silent feet to the kitchen, where she poured herself a tumbler full of white wine.

She was just lifting the glass to her lips when Breck

came after her, his feet in socks, but still shoeless. He watched her take several deep swallows and got a glass down from the cupboard for himself. He poured two fingers of neat scotch into the glass, knocked them back, and then poured two more, adding ice at last as an afterthought.

Still without a word between them, he followed her into the living room and watched her switch on several lamps. She gestured for him to sit on the couch, beneath the mermaid's picture, and she crossed to lean against the newly installed desk, where her face and upper body were shielded in the shadows. She drank several more swallows of wine and then began.

"Jeanne is my father's wife, but she's not my mother," Andrea confirmed bluntly. "I'm the child of one of my father's many mistresses. An accident, the unfortunate result of one too many nights of passion. He tried to get her to abort me, but she wouldn't, and so she died giving birth. I believe she was just barely twenty when she died. Rather young to pay such a high price for promiscuity, but then most women who have much to do with my father seem to eventually pay a pretty high price." Breck's face went taut at the soft savagery in that quiet voice.

"He brought me to Jeanne and she became my mother in every way but blood." Andrea's voice broke chokingly and then steadied. "Have you any idea what it must have cost her to take me into her home? Me, the visible proof that her husband, the man she loved, had given another woman his child? When, after more than five years of marriage, he'd never given her a child to swell her belly or rock in her arms? He'd deliberately refused her children and then brought her his bastard."

Breck watched Andrea's hands twist mindlessly, a visible lie to the calm monotone her voice had assumed. "Jeanne took me in," she continued. "She accepted me and loved me. I am her daughter, by her choice and mine. My father sowed me in another's body, but my mother, Jeanne, gave me life. Her choice was made soon after my birth, when my father placed me in her arms. My choice was made the night I left my father's house forever. It was the night after her accident, when we knew she would live . . . and how she would live."

She moved forward into the light, and he saw her face matched her tone, no flicker of emotion to break the calm mask. Only her hands betrayed her still. They twisted and clenched upon themselves.

"He told me the truth about my birth that night. I accused him of being the cause of Jeanne's accident, and he retaliated by telling me that it wasn't my concern, because she wasn't my real mother." Breck made an animal sound deep in his throat, but Andrea plowed relentlessly onward. "They'd quarreled about the blatancy of his relationship with his current secretary—no, not this one now, she's only reigned for three months so far, I believe. Jeanne was upset and she went for a drive to calm herself. The accident was an accident. The police were very specific, but she would never have been out on that freeway if it hadn't been for the quarrel. My father is morally if not physically responsible."

She drew in a shaky breath and finished, "And that is why I hate my father and love my mother Jeanne. And because she still loves him, God alone knows why, I won't let him go to jail while she's alive and could hear of it. If it weren't for her, I'd see him rot in the deepest dungeon ever dug."

Andrea gulped the remains of the wine in her glass and went back into the kitchen. Breck heard the clink of glass on glass and knew she was pouring herself another measure of wine.

There was a long silence and then he heard a drawer opening and the rattle of cutlery. He leaped convulsively off the couch and made the kitchen in five gigantic strides. Andrea regarded his precipitate arrival with astonishment. Breck looked at the sharp knife dangling from her right hand and stiffened.

Cautiously, watchfully he started toward her. "Let me have the knife, Andrea. That's no solution." Balanced on the balls of his feet, he estimated his chances of getting to her quickly enough.

She looked at him blankly. "What?" Then she seemed to realize where his eyes were so firmly fixed and she looked down at her hand. Her face took on astonished comprehension. She gestured with the knife and began to laugh. He didn't relax at all.

She tossed the knife on the counter and walked over to the refrigerator, opened it, and took out the two marinating steaks he had put in there earlier in the afternoon. "I presume these are intended for dinner tonight?" she questioned him over her shoulder. "Well, if they're cooked under the broiler with that much fat around the edges, the fat will splatter and make a terrible mess. Unless cleaning ovens is your hobby, I was going to trim the fat off and start them cooking. . . ."

She began to deftly trim the meat, wielding the wickedly sharp knife with a dazzling expertise. "I've only had cups of coffee and an appalling hamburger to eat all day and I'm hungry. You can wait to bake a potato if you want one. I'm going to broil a steak, have some green salad and some of the garlic bread I have in the freezer."

Suiting action to words, she pulled a broiler pan out of a cabinet and slapped the first steak down on its surface. She looked back at him and gestured to the second steak, which she had also trimmed. "Do you want yours cooked now too, or do you want to wait? A baked potato takes a little over an hour, and you'll have to wait awhile before you can eat."

"I'll take mine now," he responded automatically. She tossed the other steak beside the first.

"There's a boiling bag with cauliflower au gratin in the freezer." She looked his bulk up and down, evidently deciding that he needed a supplement to the menu as it had been outlined. "Do you want it?" He acquiesced readily and she began to assemble the meal, working with quick efficiency.

Without being told, Breck found plates and silverware, and following her pointing finger, pulled open a drawer to find a selection of tablecloths and napkins. Within an incredibly short time they were sitting down to a meal. Breck opened the bottle of excellent Cabernet Sauvignon he had brought to complement the steaks, but had to drink it alone. Andrea stayed with her white wine.

"I'm a wine philistine too," she commented when she refused. "I don't care for red wines particularly. In fact, I rarely drink at all, but when I do I just stick with Liebfraumilch. It was the first wine I ever tried. I've tasted others, but still prefer the Liebfraumilch. If it's not available, I have been known to switch to Green Hungarian or Chenin Blanc, but generally I just skip it. Alcohol's a fool's trap."

Andrea ate silently for a while and then continued, "So's suicide, Breck. I gather you thought I was going to slice my wrists dramatically and messily all over the kitchen awhile back. Did you think I had cause?" she said unexpectedly.

She watched the dark red run up under the bronze skin. Her attack had caught him off guard. He had been lulled by her matter-of-fact preparation of the dinner and her calm discussion of the wine. He looked at her closely and saw the opaque glitter was back, turning her gray eyes into silvery reflective mirrors, which shut him off from her thoughts. Gone was the clear, candid gaze. He could only read what she chose to let him know.

Andrea watched him from behind the shutters of her eyes. For once his face was open to her, as hers had once been to him. If it had been her innocence he had desired, then he should desire her no more, for it was well and truly dead. The past hours had killed it as surely as that sharp knife she had used on the steaks could have stilled her heart had she chosen. She was a woman now, by his making, and her girlhood had died forever in his arms.

He was wary, fearing, expecting another hysterical outburst. Her revelations had shaken him. No man could hear what she had revealed and remain untouched; uneasy at the very least and torn to the very depths if he loved the woman. Andrea didn't deceive herself. Breck didn't love her, but he desired her. Therefore he would be vulnerable to a certain extent, bound to her to at least a point because of the pleasure they had shared. She could wound him if she chose.

"I wouldn't kill myself because of you, Breck. As Lady Macbeth said, 'What's done cannot be undone.' I have gone so far for Jeanne's sake, I'll see it

130

through to the bitter end. I'll keep the bargain. See that you keep yours."

She finished her food, carried her plates to the kitchen, and loaded them in the dishwasher. She passed back through the dining area, where he still sat, toying with the remains of the wine in his glass, without sparing him even a glance. Not too much afterward he heard the water running in the shower.

When he came to bed, much later that night, she was sound asleep. She had not bothered to put on pajamas or a nightgown. Perhaps she didn't wear one normally. He didn't know, but somehow the unconcerned nakedness was an insult in itself. He yanked the sheet down from her waist, intending to shake her awake, but the outflung innocence of her hand as it rested by her head caught his attention. It looked so defenseless, the long, graceful fingers relaxed and slightly curved as a child's hand might curl during sleep.

He stood regarding the long, clean sweep of her spine and the taut arc of her buttocks. She slept on her stomach, one leg slightly drawn up and flexed, her head totally off the pillow, which was half off, half on the edge of the bed. He pulled the pillow wholly back onto the bed, but didn't tuck it back beneath her head. He went in and showered and when he came back into the bedroom, she hadn't moved an inch. He sighed, climbed into bed beside her, and pulled the covers up over them both. He switched off the bedside lamp, pulled her up against his chest, arcing around her almost protectively. It was a long time before he fell asleep, his hand cupping her breast possessively.

When he woke the next morning, the bed was cold and empty beside him. She was gone. He flung back

131

the covers and, barely stopping to pull on his jeans, strode into the living room. It was nearly eight o'clock and there were no signs of her in the kitchen, unless he counted the still slightly warm kettle of water sitting on the back burner. He headed for the studio and thrust open the door.

She didn't look up at him as he stood framed in the doorway. He could tell his presence had an effect on her—he hadn't missed the almost imperceptible stiffening of her shoulders—but her hand was steady as she continued working. It looked like the illustration for the cover of a book. She continued working for several minutes more until she had finished a row of intricate scales on the body of the medieval dragon she had been outlining in green and gold.

He walked closer and regarded the nearly completed beast. It was a roguish dragon, with a whimsical and knowing eye. He could almost swear it was preparing to wink at the rather timid-looking knight who was confronting it.

"It's for the cover of a children's book," she spoke casually, as if he had voiced the question aloud. *"Peter and Percival.* Percival's the dragon, rather on the order of Ferdinand the Bull. Peter is Sir Peter, a knight who can't seem to get the hang of accomplishing the requisite knightly endeavors in good order. When he went after the Holy Grail, he came back with a beggar's tin cup, and the maiden he rescued turned out to be the baker's daughter, who had an unfortunate partiality for her father's wares, to the detriment of her waistline and complexion. He doesn't fare much better against Percival, who is an indolent and lazy beast at best and highly averse to being impaled on the end of Peter's jousting lance. A most uncooperative and unsporting dragon, in fact."

She handed him a sheaf of ink line drawings and said, "These are the illustrations for the book itself. Even Peter's horse, Parsley, doesn't have much time for him, and the weight of Peter's armor aggravates his sciatica problem." She began to work again.

Breck leafed through the drawings and chuckled over the long-suffering resignation of the rather plump war-horse, who had a definitely unmartial gleam in his eye, especially as he reached for a tempting apple on a nearby tree, oblivious to the desires of his rider to be away in search of adventures. He admired again the deft economy of line and clean precision of her touch. Each sketch was a small, perfect work of art.

"I hope the publishing company who commissioned these has the foresight to hang on to these originals after the book is published. Someday they'll be worth a lot of money," he said dryly.

She shrugged. "They don't take long to turn out. I did these this morning. I'll have this "—she gestured at the cover painting—"finished by lunchtime and in the mail this afternoon."

He noticed the empty coffee cup on the floor beside her, but there had been no signs of a meal, either here or in the kitchen. As if she had read his mind, she said, "I think there are still some eggs in the refrigerator and there's a package of sausages in the meat drawer. Help yourself. I don't have a toaster, but I find that running it under the broiler works pretty well." She kept on working steadily.

"How long have you been working this morning?" he questioned her.

"Since six. I always do when I'm working. I'm usually too tired by evening to do commercial quality, so I work in the morning when I'm fresh." She

133

added a small touch of red to the dragon's right eye. He was definitely going to wink at Peter any minute.

"How do you like your eggs?"

She shuddered slightly. "I don't. When I must, I eat them scrambled, but when I'm working I never eat breakfast. A fried egg is an abomination, with that disgusting yellow eye staring balefully up at you. It's even worse when you break the yolk and it spreads all over the white. Ugh!"

He left before she put him off his food for good. She didn't come out until almost ten-thirty, and then only to make another cup of instant coffee. He had been working at the desk, making phone calls and dictating letters at a staccato pace for his secretary to unravel later. If it hadn't been for the occasional sound of his own voice, the apartment would have seemed deserted. No sound came from the studio, and it was the flicker of motion as she went toward the kitchen that caught his eye, rather than the silent pad of her bare feet.

Before she went back into the studio, he asked her, "Are you working against a deadline?"

All she said was, "Of sorts," and went back to work.

Andrea had been perfectly truthful. There was no hard-and-fast deadline for this particular assignment. The book was months away from publication and all that was required was reasonable speed, but the deadline was of her own making. She still intended to get through as much as was humanly possible, and now it would serve a double purpose.

More than ever she was determined to leave as soon as Jeanne died, and she would need money. It would be much harder to escape Breck's vigilance with him right here in the apartment. She hadn't planned on *that* at all! He had been correct and she foolishly naive to think he would indeed be satisfied to visit her once or twice a week and leave, but it had never entered her mind that he would *move in* with her! If it had, she might have agreed to transfer over to his apartment so that her own apartment could remain inviolate, a haven from him.

Now she would have to either resign herself to decamping with nothing but the clothes on her back when the time came, or devise some plan to circumvent his guardianship. It never entered her head to believe that he would move out after Jeanne died. His very actions negated that hope. He would leave her when *he* decided, not at the nominal end of her term of servitude.

Her studio was the only haven she had left. Breck had taken possession of the rest of her life and her surroundings. Only behind the door of her studio was she partially free of his pervasive influence.

As best she might, she intended to pretend he was not present in the apartment. She would keep to her regular schedule and habits, resolutely not allowing him to disrupt the daily routine she had evolved these several years. As for the evenings, she would meet them as they came.

She put the finishing touches on the cover illustration and left it to dry. The sheaf of drawings she interleaved with protective clean sheets and sealed in a cardboard-backed envelope. She'd pack the cover illustration the same way and then they'd all go into a larger, padded mailing bag for safe shipment.

When order was restored to the studio, she went into the bedroom to get clean clothes, intending to shower and get ready to leave for the nursing home. Breck was deep in conversation on the phone, so she escaped without hindrance to her shower. She took the precaution of dressing fully before she came back out, determined as she was to give him no opening for implementing that unmistakable gleam of desire she saw in his eyes every time he looked at her. It had been like a hand reaching out to stroke down her spine when he had looked at her from the doorway this morning as she was working. It had taken all her self-control to continue filling in the scales with a steady hand.

When she came back out, Breck was waiting for her. Sometime during the morning he had shaved and showered and was now dressed in casual slacks and an open-necked knit shirt that clung to the virile lines of his torso. What a sculptor's model he'd make, she thought, striving for detachment.

"Finished for the day?" he questioned her casually.

"With work," she agreed cautiously. "I'll grab a bite of lunch and go on to see my mother." She started to walk past him to the kitchen, but he laid a detaining hand on her arm. She froze, quietly still.

He frowned slightly but his voice was expressionless. "I'll take you to lunch. I want to meet Jeanne, so I'm going with you to the nursing home."

"You can't!" she gasped, shocked. "She's not strong enough for visitors. I won't have you upsetting her."

"I won't upset her, Andrea. Would you rather I see her alone? I can go in the morning if you'd prefer." His voice was hatefully bland.

"You know I wouldn't," she snapped. It was useless to argue with him. He bent about as much as a granite monolith! "All right, you can come," she agreed ungraciously, "but if it's one of her bad days, you won't be able to see her. I mean that, Breck." She looked fully at him, adamant.

"Of course. I'm not an unreasonable monster, Andrea," he said, chiding her gently.

The look she threw over her shoulder as she moved past him left him in no doubt that she would be willing to debate that particular point anytime he cared to. She missed the sadly wry smile that tugged at the corners of his mouth.

They lunched at a seafood restaurant where the shrimp were large and succulent, and the cocktail sauce spicy enough to take the skin off the roof of your mouth, or so the warning on the menu promised. While they ate, Andrea explained her practice of taking some present to her mother each day. She confessed that it was becoming harder every day, as Jeanne failed, to find something diverting. Breck thought for a moment and said, "I have an idea. We'll see what you think of it after lunch." He would say no more and they finished their meal, talking of other things.

He took her to a shop that sold small, motorized kinetic sculptures. She chose one that combined the soothing, ever renewing wave action of breakers on the shore with a softly shaded spectrum of changing lights. He would not let her pay for it, saying briefly, "My idea, my treat," and she left it at that.

At the nursing home it turned out to be a "good" day for Jeanne, so Andrea went in to prepare Jeanne for the idea of an unexpected visitor. To Andrea's unexpressed surprise, Jeanne did not seem at all disconcerted or curious about why Breck Carson would desire to visit her. Andrea had the uncomfortable thought that her mother would shrewdly draw her own conclusions. She could only hope that they wouldn't necessarily be the right ones.

Breck didn't let his shock at Jeanne's appearance show by so much as a muscle flicker when he came into the room. He gravely and gently took her frail hand in his large, warm one and smiled charmingly down at her. His manner was the perfect blend of concern and interest, and Jeanne visibly expanded beneath his attentive manner. He kept his visit just the right length, too, leaving before Jeanne's slender store of strength was taxed.

He told Andrea he'd see her later, leaving the impression that they had come separately but would see each other for an evening date. Andrea had to admire the finesse with which he layered so many meanings into a few simple sentences. She knew he would be waiting for her whenever she left Jeanne's room, and she shuddered to think of the impact he'd be making on the nurses while he waited for her. She sighed. A steamroller was a featherweight in comparison to Breck when he set out to accomplish something.

She spent the rest of her time with Jeanne, fielding penetrating questions concerning her feelings about Breck and the state of their relationship. To divert Jeanne from the truth, Andrea was forced to imply that she might be seriously considering marriage with Breck, but that it was really too soon for that sort of decision for either of them. Jeanne had not missed Breck's possessive air with Andrea—it was as natural as breathing for him—and Andrea was sure that he had deliberately, for reasons of his own, encouraged Jeanne's belief in the romantic qualities of their relationship.

It wouldn't do any good to tackle him about it.

138

The damage was done, and since he had met Jeanne, she would at least evaluate any rumors that got through to her from the standpoint of their possible marriage rather than an illicit liaison. For such small mercies Andrea supposed she should be grateful, since the big ones were obviously not destined to come her way.

As she had surmised, Breck had an appreciative audience around him when she finally left Jeanne. She stood watching him for a moment, unnoticed, and was puzzled by something in his attitude. He was being polite, but there was absolutely nothing more than courteous interest in his manner to the several women who were obviously trying to attract more of his attention than he was willing to give. Two of the nurses were what are colloquially called "stunners," and Andrea would have expected him to show a masculine, appreciative awareness at the very least. They might have been sixty-year-old grandmothers for all the awareness Breck was displaying.

Though none of the group had yet noticed her, and she had made no sound, Breck suddenly looked up, directly at her, and his expression changed dramatically. Now there was awareness aplenty. She felt a hot blush spread from her cheeks down her throat. He excused himself with courteous brevity and came toward her, reaching for her hand and drawing her to his side in one smooth motion. The women he had left so precipitately exchanged knowing looks and shrugs. Ah, well, Andrea deserved a little luck in her life, was their obvious conclusion.

"Are you ready to go, sweetheart?"

She shot him a fulminating look, which bounced off his bland smile. There was a suspicious twinkle at the back of his eyes, which warned her that if she provoked him, he might do something really outrageous.

"Yes, Breck. I'm ready," she replied coolly. She said good-bye to the various nurses still standing around and allowed Breck to escort her solicitously out to his car.

"Did you have to make it so obvious?" she hissed.

"Yes," he said simply. Which left her with precisely nothing to say.

They ate dinner with little conversation on either side. Andrea was still angry, and Breck seemed deep in contemplation of some not particularly felicitous thoughts. Andrea didn't try to find out what was bothering him—she seemed to come off on the short end of the stick in any exchange they had—and as far as she was concerned, he could stew in his own juice, the hotter the better.

When they were back at the apartment, Breck turned to her and said, "Go get into something comfortable; that silver-blue thing will do. I'll pour you a glass of wine. No wonder you look so tired. A schedule like the one you keep would put an elephant under." He gave her a light push toward the bedroom.

Andrea went. If he was in the kitchen pouring drinks, he wouldn't be in the bedroom watching her dress, or undress, and she was longing to "get comfortable," as he put it. She wanted nothing more than to curl up on the couch and listen to music, to escape the complications of her life for even a short while. Somehow she didn't think Breck was setting up a big seduction scene on the couch. His voice had had an impersonal, almost kindly quality, as if he suspected that too much more pressure on his part would shatter her into a thousand sharp fragments impossible to jigsaw back together again.

She didn't take any chances, though. She dressed hurriedly in the caftan. It was her favorite lounging outfit and better still, was not particularly seductive. She didn't realize that the color deepened the gray of her eyes and lent a luminescent quality to her skin, and that Breck would probably think she looked seductive in a sack.

When she went back into the living room, Breck was lounging at ease on the couch, a glass of scotch balanced on his flat stomach, staring at the ceiling. He had put on Saint-Saëns's Third Symphony and was keeping time with one waving forefinger. As before, he seemed to sense when she entered the room, because he turned to look at her, though any sound of her entrance would have been covered by the music.

He rose to his feet, picked up her glass of wine, and walked over to hand it to her. She took it, carefully avoiding contact with his fingers. He didn't comment, but merely took her free wrist and led her back to the couch, standing before her until she sat down. She sat and contemplated her wine.

Breck sat down next to her, positioning himself comfortably in the angle of the couch back and arm, and then carefully pulled her back to lean against him, supporting her in turn in the angle of his chest and arm. She held herself rigidly for a while, but her spine began protesting at the unnatural strain, so she finally relaxed against him, wiggling a bit to get comfortable.

"Now drink your wine and listen to the music," his voice drawled in her ear as he laid the side of his cheek against her temple.

It was actually pleasant. He made no demands of her, just held her gently as though he enjoyed being next to her, and she felt her tension and apprehension gradually drain away. When he got up to change the music and replenish her wine, she waited patiently for him to return and then went back into his arms without protest.

The idyll lasted for several hours, until at last her eyelids grew lead-weighted and she began to yawn, half stifled little cat yawns. Breck chuckled and lifted her to her feet. He pointed her toward the bathroom and said quietly, "Go get ready for bed, Andrea. I'll lock up and turn off the music. Go on, scoot."

Whether he was being tactful or not, he didn't come into the bedroom until she had had plenty of time to drag out and don an old granny gown, high-necked and voluminous, that she only wore in the dead of winter. As he had surmised, normally she slept nude, but it was one thing to appear naked before him in anger and quite another to contemplate doing so tonight, she found.

When he came into the bedroom, he caught her just climbing into bed. At the sight of her cloth-enshrouded form a startled oath burst from him and he began to laugh. "What in hell's name have you got on?"

"It's my nightgown," she asserted with precarious dignity, her eyes beginning to spark.

"I thought it was a tent. Take it off."

"No!"

"All right," he said mildly. She gaped at him, and he began to take off his own clothes. It was the work of moments and she was still standing staring at him in shock when he finished and advanced toward her. She began to back away automatically and ran up

142

against the edge of the bed, which she had forgotten was directly behind her. She started to topple backward, overbalanced, until he reached forward and gently pulled her back upright. When she was steady on her feet again, he grasped the gown in his two hands at the neck opening and calmly split it from neck to hem with one rending motion. He pulled the ruined gown the rest of the way off of her and dropped it on the floor.

The rest of the night was a duplicate of the previous one, except that this time there was no pain before ecstasy. She resisted him passively until she could do so no longer. He was patient and persevering, and he wooed her with an attention to her responses, building an edifice of passion slowly but thoroughly. At last he tipped her over the edge of delight and only then did he follow after her, to finish holding her tightly, gasping and spent, a close tangle of welded bodies. The last thing Andrea clearly remembered was Breck pulling the covers up over their intertwined bodies and tucking the sheet and blanket firmly around them both.

The pattern of their days and nights was set for the next several weeks, except that no more of her gowns suffered the fate of the first. She slid silently from bed each morning, thinking him still asleep, because his arms always slackened to release her. She didn't know he watched her exit from the room each morning through slitted eyes, enjoying the unconsciously sensuous sway of her hips as she left him to shower and begin her day's work in the studio. He would rise an hour later to shower, shave, and eat his solitary breakfast.

The rest of the morning followed much the same pattern as the first, she in the haven of the studio and he at the desk. He gradually managed to extend the time she allowed herself for a midmorning break, but it was subtly done, each extra minute added with stealthy caution.

Andrea was aware that Breck seemed to have taken over the ordering of her life, but she was powerless to stop him. She could not keep him from visiting Jeanne, and he went many times with her. Even on the afternoons that he went to the office instead of to visit Jeanne with her, they still shopped together for her daily present. He dropped her at the nursing home and picked her up, and no demur seemed to dissuade him. They ate lunch and dinner together, sometimes out, sometimes at the apartment. He was handy in the kitchen and, better yet, unselfconscious about it.

They went to the framers together to pick out a frame for Breck's picture and Andrea watched Kevin's eyebrows rise when she walked in beside Breck. She met his speculative glances with a stony stare of her own, and he wisely made no unfortunate remarks. Breck didn't miss the little byplay and it seemed to amuse him no end. Andrea was icily civil the rest of the afternoon. Fortunately it was one of the days Breck chose to go to the office, so she was not forced to dissimulate before Jeanne.

That night, Breck took her to another play, again a first night, but when he asked if she wanted to go to the cast party, she declined. He laughed and they went dancing afterward instead. The next morning she overslept, and Breck took care to confirm her erroneous belief that he had been asleep on previous mornings when she had "escaped" to the studio, by making thorough and prolonged love to her. This time she actively fought him, but the end result was the same.

The days passed. The silent struggle continued. She resisted; he ruthlessly overcame. In itself, her continued resistance was a victory of sorts, but Andrea knew only that she seemed to lose every encounter with Breck. He blocked every bid for freedom she made and eroded the areas she tried to keep separate from him. He began coming into the studio at odd times, standing quietly near her, watching her as she worked. It was nerve-racking, but when he asked her if having him watch made her nervous, pride forced her to deny it. He came in more often.

The dichotomy of her emotions was tearing her apart. Her mind was again at war with her body, and the conflict was like to destroy her. The fact that she was Breck's mistress was a raw acid wound across the fabric of her self-respect, but the touch of his hands on her body and the stroke of his lips and tongue at her breast made the time of passive resistance each night grow ever shorter. Someday soon, unless she could get away, she would come eagerly to his arms and something would die forever within her. The thought terrified her.

The time of stasis was coming to an end. Breck was having to spend more afternoons at the office, and Jeanne's final days began to run out with merciful rapidity. Breck had been unable to accompany her to see Jeanne for the past four days, and Andrea's talk with the doctor confirmed her private belief that the end was very near.

She obtained the doctor's promise that any inquiries about Jeanne's condition would continue to be met with the standard formula, "as well as can be expected," and she promised to inform her father of her mother's steadily worsening condition herself. Her plans were made. All she needed was the chance to implement them.

When Breck picked her up that afternoon from the nursing home, she knew something was about to happen. He was in a black mood, and she felt a burgeoning hope. Perhaps whatever was its cause could be turned to her advantage. If he was preoccupied with business problems, whatever they were, might his vigilance lessen just that necessary fraction?

Hope made her all the more cautious, and when Breck asked about her mother during their evening meal, she replied warily. "She's much the same. Failing more rapidly, of course, each day just that much weaker and more ready to go. Dr. Scofield increased her medication again and she's able to sleep somewhat. We don't talk much anymore . . . I just sit and hold her hand most of the time."

"I see," he said thoughtfully. "Can he give you an educated guess about how much longer?"

She was instantly alert, but careful not to let it show. "A week, two weeks, a month at the outside," she answered dully. "He thinks the increased sedation will slow the end somewhat, because she rests more, has more surcease from the constant pain, but as I told you before, it also weakens her heart. When she reaches the critical point, it'll be over very quickly." Now she uttered a deliberate lie. "His best estimate is about another two weeks, but . . ." she shrugged and spread her hands helplessly.

"I see," he repeated again and ran an agitated hand through his hair. He reached over and grasped her hands, commanding her attention. "Andrea, I'm going to have to fly to New York for three days. I've

146

put off the trip as long as I can, but it can't wait any longer. I'm booked on a flight tomorrow morning."

"Oh," was all she could say, but deep inside a surety was born. This was to be her chance. Call it fate, call it belated redress, but sometime within that three-day span she knew, with a deep, undeniable instinct, that the time would come for Jeanne and for herself. She looked down at the clasped hands to hide her expression, not looking up until she was sure she could control her eyes.

"Andrea, if I thought the end was near, I'd stay, no matter what. I know you think you're prepared for this, and I know it will be nothing but a release for Jeanne, but I don't want you to go through this alone."

Her eyes flew up to meet his and there was nothing but sincerity and concern in the blue fire of his gaze. It was nearly her undoing. Suddenly she wanted to throw herself against him and ask him to stay, to be her bulwark and her comfort in the dark days she knew were ahead.

"Do you want me to stay, Andrea? Do you agree with the doctor's estimate?"

His voice was so gentle, so softly concerned, that she nearly gave in. Tenderness was much harder to fight than passion. Then she caught sight of her ring-less left hand and her resolve stiffened. He was her lover, not her husband. She was his mistress, not his wife.

The eyes she lifted again from their clasped hands brimmed with tears and her voice was husky. "I agree with the doctor's estimate, Breck. Go on to New York. Jeanne and I will be all right while you're in New York."

Then she cried. He scooped her up and carried her

over to the couch, where he sat for a long time, holding her close, letting her cry out all the accumulated tensions and regrets. Though he didn't know it, she cried too for the times she would not be able to cry in his arms after Jeanne was gone. Finally, exhausted and hiccuping like a child, she was able to stop.

He carried her into the bedroom and undressed her, tucking her into the bed with tender care. He brought a cold washcloth to bathe her face and left her for a while in the dimly lighted room until he had taken care of the dishes and locked up for the night. When he came to her that night, she met him at last with an unreserved passion to match his own.

It was her farewell to him and an unspoken avowal of feelings she would not name, dared not put into words for the sake of her sanity. He whispered that he wanted her, needed her, called her darling and sweetheart in the darkness, but never beloved. In the silence of her heart she named him love, but the words never crossed her lips.

They made love again early the next morning with a passionate savagery Andrea would have thought herself incapable of. Last night had been farewell. This was for memory.

CHAPTER SIX

Breck packed, and she made his breakfast, even going so far as to eat a slice of bacon to keep him company while he consumed the two sunny-side-up eggs she had cooked for him. She had arranged them side by side and had placed a curved slice of bacon beneath the two eggs to simulate a crooked mouth. She burst into a peal of laughter at his expression when he first looked down at his plate, and laughed again when he immediately ate the bacon and shoved the eggs around on the plate.

He grinned at her and commented, "It might be safer to stick to cereal when you're making the breakfast. Good thing I don't have a hangover this morning!"

She drove him to the airport and waited until his plane was airborne, a rapidly diminishing dot in the sky.

When she got back to the apartment, she called the nursing home and received the report she had expected. Methodically she set about packing. There really wasn't much she wanted to take with her: clothes, her paintings and business papers, and the two sketches she had made of Breck. She would do an oil of him someday when the pain had faded a little.

When she had packed all she planned to take with her, she took several loads down to the car, filling the trunk and locking it. The rest could wait. She stopped by her bank on the way to the nursing home and came out with a sizeable bundle of traveler's checks. She also filled the car with gas and had the attendant check the oil, water, and tires. She was ready.

The night was very long. She sat by Jeanne's bed, leaving it only for the length of time it took her to call her father. She resolutely ignored the feminine voice she could hear questioning him in the background and said quietly, "Jeanne's dying. Do you want to come?"

They kept vigil, one on each side of the bed, each holding a wasted hand. Just before dawn, Jeanne woke once more from her stupor, but it was to Andrea she looked as her eyes dimmed and blanked. It was Andrea who closed her eyes and pulled the sheet over the peaceful, pain-free face, and then called the nurse.

Andrea and Devlin walked outside, into the corridor, together. Andrea turned to face him, her expression unrevealing. "Good-bye, Devlin." She turned to go.

He caught her arm. She looked down at his hand grasping her elbow and her lip curled. He removed his hand as though her arm had suddenly flared white hot. "I'll arrange the funeral," he said. "I'll let you know the time and details later."

"Don't bother. I won't be there."

Shock aged his face. "What do you mean you won't be there?" he croaked.

"I'm leaving town. I won't be back for the funeral. You'll have to play the grieving husband without my supporting role. Perhaps your secretary can wear the mourning black in my place."

"You aren't going to attend your mother's funeral?" He seemed to find the thought incomprehensible.

"No. I honored her in life. She has no need of my presence now. I leave the public mourning to you." Bitter scorn dripped from her voice.

"You can't leave town!" Naked panic hoarsened his throat. "What about Breck? You can't run out on him!"

"Amnesty's over, Devlin." She smiled with wolfish enjoyment. "You really are despicable, you know. Willing to barter my body to escape the consequences of your own actions. Well, understand me, and remember what I say. What I did, I did for Jeanne, to save her one more bit of pain in the hell she endured for those long, long years. She's gone now, and I'm free. No man will ever use me again for any reason whatsoever, and I hope Breck Carson puts you in jail for the rest of your life. And if he does, I hope you live to be a hundred years old."

She drew in a deep breath and said with stunning emphasis, in a dead-level, icy cold voice, "The worst curse I can think of to lay upon you is that you get everything you deserve."

She turned and walked away from him, head high, and never looked back or faltered.

Andrea drove back to the apartment, brought the rest of her things out to the car, locked the door behind her, and went down in the elevator for the last time. She left no note for Breck. There was nothing to say.

She drove for several hours, not really caring about her direction for the moment, and stopped at

151

the first motel she came to. After she had registered, she went into the impersonal room, carrying only an overnight case. She made sure the door was securely locked behind her, dropped the case on one of the beds, and took off all of her clothes. Then she crawled into the nearest bed and slept the clock around.

When she woke the next morning, she felt physically better, but there was a persistent ache deep in her throat, as though she were perpetually on the verge of tears but unable to cry. She wished she could cry, but she knew if she did, the tears wouldn't be for Jeanne. They would be for Breck. They would be for herself.

He would have heard of Jeanne's death by now. She knew he would have made arrangements to be notified of just such an event, not trusting her to get in touch with him, as she had not. He would not be surprised to find her gone. The fact that she had not called to tell him about Jeanne would prepare him for her flight, and she rather imagined that Devlin would be in for a very uncomfortable time when Breck came back.

Breck wouldn't prosecute Devlin, even though Andrea was now no longer his mistress, and technically their bargain was at an end. She had merely taunted Devlin with the possibility to see him squirm a bit. Breck would see that Devlin never again had any position of influence, and the odor of theft would waft about him for the rest of his life. That would be punishment in part, but never enough, never enough. Time and old age would do the rest, she supposed, and with that she dismissed Devlin Thomas from her mind.

Breck would look for her, and do a thorough job

of it, Andrea was sure. He would not easily let go of what was "his" for as long as he wanted it. He was not yet ready to let *her* go, but for the sake of her self-respect she had to go, to cut him out of her life and do it thoroughly.

Andrea showered and changed into comfortable clothes. She had a long way to go. While she ate her way through a large stack of waffles and the side order of bacon that came with it, she pored over the maps she had extracted from the glove compartment of her car. After she had determined exactly where she was, she could plot the most direct route to her destination. She was happy to discover that she hadn't come too far out of her route, and it would be comparatively simple to reach the interstate she needed.

As Andrea had expected, Breck had indeed made arrangements to insure that he be kept informed of Jeanne's condition. Andrea's intervention with the doctor had thrown his plans awry and he did not hear of Jeanne's death until his secretary called him out of a meeting in New York at midafternoon. She secured her job by that one act of initiative, because it was through her love of gossip that she was able to pluck the news off the grapevine.

Miss Jenkins was a romantic at heart. She knew that there was a *relationship* between Breck Carson and Andrea Thomas. She also knew that Breck had fired, without reference, two men he had overheard discussing that relationship crudely. Witnesses who saw the incident said that it had been only through some thin tendril of self-control on Breck's part that the two men escaped being broken into pieces by a ragingly furious Breck. No one dared protest the summary firings, least of all the two men involved. They considered themselves lucky to have escaped whole-skinned and were content to seek work elsewhere.

When Miss Jenkins heard that Mr. Thomas's wife had finally died, via the consequent speculation about the possible change in status of his erstwhile secretary—she had stayed to work for the company when Devlin was "retired"—she immediately began to try to reach Breck. She waded through layers of secretaries, endlessly repeating her refrain of family emergency until she penetrated even the board meeting.

Breck thanked her sincerely for her efforts. He'd find out later why his other sources hadn't notified him, but right now his primary efforts were directed toward getting hold of Andrea and getting back to her. He preempted the nearest secretary, who happened to belong to the company treasurer, and set her to arranging his flight connections. He spent fruitless minutes dialing the phone at the apartment and listening to it ring. He would not let himself think of possibilities when there was no answer.

When his flight connections were completed, he had the secretary contact the nursing home, but she could find out nothing there other than the bare fact of the confirmation of Jeanne's death and that both her husband and her daughter had been with her at the end. Breck's face was a savage mask.

There was time for nothing more if he were to make the flight the secretary had managed to book for him. There had been only one seat left on the plane and it would be his.

Breck went directly to the apartment when he arrived. When he went in the door, his eyes went immediately to the wall over the couch. His face twisted and his eyes closed in an intense spasm of pain. The wall was blank. The mermaid was gone.

With dragging steps he went into the bedroom and pulled back the closet curtain. Only his clothes hung on the rails. He sank down on the edge of the bed, his head dropped in his hands, palms against his forehead.

Andrea was faring a little better. She was fortunate enough to locate a small beach house at a reasonable rent. The mermaid had returned to the sea, or at least as close to it as was humanly possible.

The house was elderly, but had been well maintained and the silvery, weathered boards that sided it pleased Andrea's aesthetic eye. A grass-spotted sand dune ran right up under the front porch, which was raised on stilts. The house was compact, but it had two bedrooms upstairs, both of which had a marvelous view of the sea in all of its moods. She chose the larger one for her studio, and since the house was only sparsely and partially furnished, did not have too much rearranging to do to give herself the maximum amount of working space.

She didn't hang the pictures she had brought with her. She turned the mermaid and her watery world to the wall and left her there. For the first week that she was in the house she did no work at all. She walked the beach, ate when she had to, and slept when she could. After a week, she was sleeping better and her appetite had improved. Something is better than nothing.

Andrea was sitting in her favorite spot overlooking the ocean when she decided it was time to begin working again. She had come every day to this spot to watch the thrashing waves tear themselves to bits on the rock teeth that stuck, like jagged incisors, from a spine of rock lying offshore a hundred yards away. The thunder of the surf answered something stormy and dark that churned in the pit of her stomach.

Today, at last, she felt an easing and the tears began to run silently down her cheeks. She sat there for a long while, fat tears plopping with salty splashes to mingle with the ocean spray on her clothes. When she rose, she felt empty and drained. Not healed . . . only time and work could do that for her now, but *ready* to be healed. She had exorcised the festering hate and those tears had carried away the last remains of the malignant hatred that had stunted her emotional growth and had twisted her and her relationships with other people. For the first time she was truly free . . . and believed it.

She walked back to the house with a lighter step and thrown-back shoulders. Now she had a plan of action. She had letters to write and a pattern of living to begin. She had lived an abnormal life for so long that she was going to need time to throw off old habits and routines. She had skipped a normal part of her adolescence and had been catapulted by circumstances into a maturity, lopsided though it was, that had left her unbalanced, mature in some areas, dangerously adolescent in others. It was time to remedy that.

She wrote her letters, informing her various selected clients of her new address and adjuring them to release her location to *no* one. She reinforced that instruction with the implied threat that, were her privacy breached, she would do no further work for the offender. She was explicit enough and her work was valued so highly that she had no fears that they would do anything but guard her privacy with zealous attention.

She sent a letter to the owners of her apartment building to acquaint them with her decision about the apartment. When these letters were done, she felt such a sensation of relief that she nearly bubbled with it. The old life was gone and though it would be hard, she was determined to build herself another. The healing had begun.

For the first week after she began to work again, she concentrated on her commercial accounts. She wanted to have a firm financial base established before she began to paint seriously, and too, she was not ready to undergo the emotional trauma that such paintings, especially the ones she knew must be painted, were going to cause her.

She gave herself time. There was no urgency. The time for decisions would come, to be sure, but this was a time of renewal and rebuilding, and she must do it right. For the first time in her recent life, she was at peace within herself.

She also began, slowly, to enter into the life of the small community closest to her house. She stopped to chat at the small grocery store where she bought her supplies and at the post office/general store, where she bought everything else and picked up her mail. From there also she sent off her completed commissions, and thus satisfied general curiosity about her means of livelihood.

She knew she was an object of curiosity to the small community, an attractive single young woman who lived alone and had discouraged any but the most fleeting personal contacts when she first arrived. She revealed nothing of her personal history, except that her mother had recently died and she had felt in need of a change of scene from unhappy associations. She set no time limit on the duration of her stay.

This satisfied the inquisitive and cut off most of the probing questions out of tact because of her recent bereavement. The rest she took care of with a level, icy stare, which had a tendency to dry the words in the mouth of the importunate inquisitor. Andrea at her most quelling could be formidable indeed. She was gravely friendly but not ebullient, and her reticence had the not surprising effect of imbuing her with a tantalizing air of mystery.

The alert bachelors noted this exciting addition to the feminine portion of the population, and she began to receive invitations to beach parties and other local affairs. Most she declined, but she did, after much thought, accept a few, those where she did not feel the need for an escort. She mingled well but allowed none of the unattached males at the various parties to attach themselves to her permanently. She came alone and left alone, even if she was never alone while actually at the parties themselves.

When she had lived in the beach house for a month, Andrea set up her easel and began to paint. The first one she did was the view from her favorite spot overlooking the ocean. She put into it all the turmoil and torment that had racked her as she had sat looking out at the shredded waves. It was a wild and disturbing picture and tended to make those who viewed it in later years rather uneasy, although they couldn't define just why. Critics considered it an anomaly in the body of the majority of her work, but that only made it more desirable. She never sold it and rarely exhibited it, but when it was on public view, it invariably commanded attention and persistent offers.

She devoted less and less time to her commercial art, accepting only book and cover illustrations and a few selected, very lucrative commissions, which took little actual time to complete. She lived very simply and found her wardrobe, as it stood, to be very adequate to the small social demands she placed on it.

At last she began to accept an occasional date for dinner or a movie from among her more persistent admirers, but rarely with the same man twice in a row. None of her escorts tried to breach that intangible air of personal isolation. She could be an entertaining companion for an evening, but the slightest hint of any personal element or sexual overture on the part of the man brought an impenetrable, invisible barrier thudding down. She was prepared to be a companion, perhaps even a friend, but not a girl friend.

There was a woman's awareness in her eyes, but none tried to take advantage of it. Andrea was secretly amused many times, though not a flicker of it appeared on her face. She was a woman. Breck had made her one. She had known passion and had satisfied a man's desire, as he had hers, she wryly acknowledged to herself. She was no longer protected by that invisible air of innocence, and her escorts unconsciously reacted to the loss of that indefinable defensive barrier.

The loss of innocence had not left her undefended, however. Her experience with Breck had stripped her of innocence, but in its place he had left her with an awareness of the powers her woman's body wielded over men. Eve's knowledge, Lilith's knowledge:

blood-deep, bone-bred heritage of any woman who understands her own nature and has come to terms with it. Andrea was coming to terms with herself and if the maturation process was at times painful, it was also inexorable.

By the end of the fifth month, Andrea had a respectable number of canvases completed, almost enough for a small show. She was tanned and vitally alive, and although there was an unmistakable maturity about her, in some indefinable way she was also younger and more carefree than she had been since her early teen-age days, as though she had somehow managed to recapture a portion of her lost innocence.

It was time to begin the picture of Breck. It was the final test she set herself, the proof of complete healing. Like the exorcism of a haunting ghost, she would purge her subconscious of any lingering traces that could conceivably come between her and the life she hoped would someday be hers.

She had known this day would have to come and she had gathered her strength to meet the challenge she set herself. She had gone out with other men, though she had carefully allowed none of them to exact more from her than she was willing to give. This was her period of mourning, her metaphorical wearing of black, both for the loss of Jeanne and of her own girlhood. With the completion of the picture she now intended to paint, she would know whether it had come to an end.

She began to take long walks along the beach again. The summer had fled and the salt spray that whipped her skin had added a chill bite. Several storms, harbingers of winter's approaching inclemency, lashed at the little house. It creaked and groaned and the windows rattled like chattering teeth, but apart from an icy draft or two, which sent Andrea to the general store for a tube of caulk, it remained the snug haven it had been for her months of exile.

She withdrew from the social life of the town once more, retreating into the impersonality of her first few weeks residence. She pleaded pressure of work, not wishing to have to resort to incivility, and was adamant about refusing all invitations, no matter how pressing.

Once again she ate, slept, and took long walks, but with a difference. This time she worked on the picture as well. It was as painful as she had feared it was going to be, and it took her almost a month to finish it.

She finished it late in the afternoon and when she had laid on the last brush stroke, she paused for a moment and then turned away. She gathered together her materials and began to clean up, working mechanically and consciously avoiding looking at the picture. Tomorrow would be soon enough.

She fixed herself a scratch meal and then took a postprandial cup of coffee with her out to the porch, which faced the ocean. She pulled up a battered mission rocker, as weathered as the wood of the house, to within comfortable distance of the railing. She sat down, cradling the warmth of the cup between her hands and balancing the base of the cup on her stomach. She propped her feet up on the railing and tilted the chair back on its rockers.

The nearly full moon was rising from the watery depths of the ocean and she watched the silvery path spread across the gently heaving bosom of the ocean as it lay beyond the sand dunes. The ceaseless wash

161

of the waves formed a hypnotic accompaniment in the night and she let her eyes flicker shut. She was so tired.

The next morning she rose early and went for a short morning swim. The water was breathtakingly cold, but it left her tingling and awake. Suddenly she was ravenously hungry. She fried bacon and scrambled eggs and ate them with relish. There was no pain from her memories and when she climbed the stairs, it was with a firm, unhurried tread. Her hand on the doorknob of her studio was steady and her face, as she stood before the painting, was calm and composed.

She looked at the canvas for a long time, assimilating the total message it had for her. When she turned away at last, it was with a sigh of relief. She was truly free. The long days and nights had been worth it. Disillusion and sorrow had scoured her deeply, as the potter's hands hollow the cup spinning on his wheel, but the capacity of the vessel is enlarged by the oft painful treatment. The long months of voluntary isolation had purged her of the bitterness and hatred. Old loves and old hates had drained away, leaving her empty, ready to be filled with a new, untainted emotion.

Love could never be the innocent unfolding it might have been. Too much had happened that could never be wiped away; her dreams had been too ruthlessly smashed to be put back together in their old forms. Her gills had metamorphosized into lungs and her old environment was forever barred to her. It was time to build herself a new life.

There was no reason to delay. She notified the real estate agent who managed the rental of the house that she would be vacating the cottage within the week. She had the car serviced and made her good-byes while she waited for it. She had deliberately kept the threads that bound her to this place tenuous. She had always known this was an interim, an interlude between her old life and the new one she would fashion for herself. She had shed her old responsibilities and the new ones she was ready to assume would be those of her own choosing, not those thrust upon her by events she could not control.

Once again she packed her clothes, but without the haste that had governed her earlier departure. Now there was no hurry. She was not running away ever again. She arranged for shipment of the majority of the canvases, taking only two new ones in the car with her, plus the ones she had brought with her.

Two days after she had stood before Breck's picture, she locked the door of the beach house for the last time, got in the car, and drove away. There were no backward glances.

Breck parked his car and got out wearily. Six long months had passed since Jeanne's death. If Andrea had mentally characterized him as an ancient Norse warrior, he was now a warrior for whom the battle had not gone well. Lines of strain were graven deep in his face. His mouth was tightly drawn, evidence of the exercise of now habitual control; a man who bears suffering because he has no way to alleviate it.

Andrea had been correct. He had looked for her most thoroughly. Every avenue had been explored, each ending in stone walls or a welter of false alarms. Andrea had chosen her clients well. None would jeopardize their relationship with her and release her new address. There were no secretaries to be suborned, because she had forsightedly provided that knowledge of her whereabouts be confined to one or two high-level executives of the departments concerned, and there were no return addresses for prying eyes to note. She had even contrived that the postmarks be blurred by smiling sweetly at the mail clerk each time she mailed off a package.

It was bitterly clear that she had planned every move well in advance, even to making sure that no news about the deterioration in Jeanne's condition was released. She had ably fulfilled her vow. When Jeanne died, she cut with ruthless precision all the ties he had sought to bind around her. He had no doubt that even had no fortuitous—from her point of view—business trip intervened, she would somehow have contrived to escape his enmeshing net.

The bait had not been sufficient to trap the mermaid after all. She had swum tracelessly back into the depths, leaving the man empty armed on the shore. Had she gone back mortally wounded by her experiences on land? Had the time she had spent breathing air forever destroyed her ability to live in the tranquil deeps? What price was *she* paying for *his* arrogant decision to snare the mermaid, regardless of the cost to her?

He had hoped to bind her with passion, to lock her with him in a mutual web of enchantment, but had he only succeeded in opening her perceptions to the sensual pleasures and potentials of the flesh? Would she sate the hungers he had aroused in her innocent body with another man? The thought of her in another man's arms clawed his gut with savage persistence. She had responded to him in spite of her hatred. Would she respond to another out of love or even a mere desire for comfort?

Was she pregnant? He had taken no precautions

against it and had found no evidence that she had thought of doing so either. In fact, he scathingly reminded himself, he had hoped to make her pregnant, to bind her to himself in that way. She would marry him for the sake of the child, he had reasoned.

Was she now growing large with his child? He knew her well enough to know that if she were, she would bear it and raise it. Would he ever know whether a child of his body walked the earth? What if she died of it? Women did. Her mother had. In spite of doctors and hospitals and modern medicine, women still died giving birth to the fruit of a man's lust for the warmth and wonder of their bodies. Andrea was slim-hipped. What if? What if?

He shook his head, seeking to chase away the phantasm, guilt born, which had haunted him for six months, long, aching, lonely months. He still turned in the night, reaching automatically to enfold her warm, lithe body, finding only cold, empty space. It was slowly killing him and he had only himself to blame. Like a greedy, spoiled child, he had reached for that which was not his, but which he desired above everything he had ever wanted. Mea culpa, he reminded himself wryly.

The elevator shuddered to a halt and his footsteps echoed hollowly in the hall. He inserted the key and walked in the front door of the apartment, his eyes going automatically to the empty space over the couch. It was sheer reflex now, compulsive and conditioned.

He took another step, tugging to loosen his tie, before his brain registered the message his eyes were telling him. He stopped dead still, afraid to move, afraid even to breathe. His lids dropped down over his eyes, sealing him within a black, still world, a world in which a small, wavering, ever so fragile pinpoint of light began to burn. After a moment that seemed eons long, he opened his eyes slowly. Perhaps he had finally gone mad. "Hope deferred maketh the heart sick". . . and perhaps the eyes hallucinate?

The picture was there, hanging in its accustomed place. He walked jerkily over to it, his hand outstretched to touch the surface, where the mermaid flirted with visibility. His fingers met the reality of canvas and paint, dragging slightly as he swept them over the painted texture.

He stepped back from the couch and swung to face the rest of the room. His head lifted alertly, straining to catch a whisper of sound. The stillness was complete, not even the stirring of an air current to carry a drift of the presence of another human being.

Had she come, and finding him still resident, gone? No! She must still be here. He strode into the kitchen. Empty. Their bedroom next.

There was a new painting hanging over the bed, but the room was empty. He saw three suitcases on the other side of the bed and he stalked over to investigate. From the weight of one he hefted experimentally, he decided they hadn't been unpacked. A quick check behind the curtain of the closet confirmed his guess. Only his own clothes hung there.

That left the studio. The door was closed, but that was not unusual. He kept it that way. It had been her sanctuary, the place she had done her best to keep free from his presence. He had known what it had meant to her even when he deliberately invaded it while she worked. He castigated himself as he had so many times before. He had been unwilling to allow her even a corner free from his imprint, forcing himself here as he had forced himself on her unwilling body.

His hand turned the doorknob, and the door swung open at his touch. At first he thought she was not here either. The room was quiet and there was no flicker of motion to draw the eye. Her easel stood again in the center of the room, a canvas propped on its support. He could not see its subject; the back of the canvas faced the door.

She was standing by one of the windows, looking down at the ground. You could see the parking area from that window. She had watched him park his car and enter the building. She knew he was here, but she didn't turn to face him immediately.

Breck drank in the sight of that slender figure clad in shirt and jeans with ravenous eyes. She stood in profile, backlighted by the window. She did not carry his child. That was immediately obvious from the slim perfection of that narrow waist and flat stomach.

There was no perceptible tension in that lithe figure as she turned gracefully to confront him. There was a new maturity and calm certainty on her face, and no surprise evident as she looked coolly and directly at him. He could not read her expression at all, save that it held no hate or fear.

"Hello, Breck."

Her voice was just the same, low-toned and slightly husky, with a soft slip of syllables, which nevertheless kept a precise pronunciation so that each word remained clean and distinct. He watched her lips move and then be still. Was there just the trace of a small smile on them in repose?

"Andrea." He could say nothing more. His voice

clogged in his throat. So many questions to ask, but for now he was content to look and look again.

Andrea read his face with wondering eyes. The time had not been easy for him and the marks six months had clawed in his face were plainly and deeply carved. I'll bet he's made life hell at the office. I wonder how Miss Jenkins is faring? she mused silently.

"You came back." The statement was a question. Breck's voice was dry in his throat.

"It's my apartment, Breck," she reminded him noncommitally. "I've paid the rent for it these past six months."

"I know."

Every month the travelers checks had come in to the apartment owners, impersonal and untraceable. Apart from that initial letter, which informed the landlord that she wished to maintain the tenantcy of the apartment on a month to month basis for an unspecified length of time, there had been no further communication with her. They had been instructed to contact a certain publisher if there were any messages concerning rent increases or other matters pertaining to the apartment, and a message would be transmitted to her.

Breck had contacted the publisher and requested that they transmit a message from him. They refused, explaining that she had told them specifically to transmit only those messages relating to the apartment, of the nature she had outlined in her letter to the landlord.

The import was brutally clear. She wanted no communication with her past life. She was cutting herself completely adrift from prior associations, and only the frail link of the month to month rental and those regular checks tied her in any way to old affiliations. That link she could sever at any time, and might. She had taken everything of personal significance with her when she went, leaving only haunting phantoms behind to torment him.

So he had stayed. He slept in the bed that they had shared and reached for her in the night. He ate at the table and sat on the couch and worked at the desk. Each day when he came in he looked at the spot where the picture had hung, never expecting it to be filled again.

Andrea moved toward him with the same elegant economy of motion that he remembered so well. His heart leapt in his throat, but she merely passed by him, out of the studio, carefully not touching him in any way. He followed hastily, unwilling to let her out of his sight for an instant.

She went into the kitchen, where she began to heat water in her teakettle for coffee. She got out one cup, and then glanced at him over her shoulder. "Do you want some instant coffee? If you want perked, you'll have to do it yourself."

"I'll take instant."

She got down another cup and spooned coffee crystals into both cups, adding sugar and milk to hers as she waited for the water to come to a boil. When the kettle began to whistle, she poured the water in, stirred both brews with the same spoon, and handed him the cup with the unsweetened black coffee. She picked up her own and wandered out into the living room.

She surveyed the room and commented, "You haven't made any changes. Do you still have your own apartment?"

"Yes," he replied warily. "I imagine that the dust

169

is inches thick there by now, but I've kept it. I own the building. You never saw it, but it's the penthouse apartment."

She nodded, unsurprised. She had never made any effort to inquire into his business dealings or holdings. She knew he was wealthy and had many interests, but all of their relationships had been on such an intensely personal level that what he did with the part of his life separate from her had never had a chance to enter into their relationship. It had been a side issue, unimportant at the time.

She sipped her coffee thoughtfully. "I'm not your mistress anymore, Breck."

She said it so casually, so quietly, that it took a moment for the impact of her words to strike him. When they did, he blenched, his body jerking slightly with the invisible blow her words dealt.

Then his eyes narrowed and he braced himself. He would fight for what he wanted. He would not give her up.

Andrea watched his reaction. She saw the effect her words had on him, saw him absorb the blow, accept it, and began to prepare to contest her pronouncement. Her eyes grew frostily chill. Had he learned nothing during the six months she had been gone? Did he still think to force her to his will?

"What have you been doing these past months, Andrea? You look very well." Breck kept his voice level and calm with immense effort. She didn't look well, she looked lovely. She was relaxed and tanned and so heart-stoppingly beautiful that she made his very bones ache with the effort he was making to control himself. He wanted to hold her and kiss her and bury himself so deeply in her that they became one, indissolubly.

"I've been painting," she informed him dryly. "I have almost enough canvases for a show. Another month or so and I'll be ready. I took your advice, you see. I decided to concentrate on my serious painting."

"But where were you?" he insisted. He felt a driving need to know in detail all about her life these last months. Had she left someone important behind her when she came back to the apartment? Would she return once a show was arranged?

"I went to a small town on the Carolina coast and rented a beach house. I've been there the whole time." She smiled slightly to herself and said deliberately, "It was a very friendly little town. Everyone was most kind and they made me feel welcome."

"I'll bet," he muttered to himself, black jealousy gnawing deeply into him.

Andrea turned away, lifting her coffee cup to her mouth to hide her twitching lips. Still the same possessive Breck. She began to wander aimlessly around the living room, straightening a cushion on the couch, running a forefinger across the surface of the desk and arching an eyebrow at the dust that adhered to her bare fingertip. The apartment was clean and tidy, but Breck was obviously not a white-glove inspector. She wondered if he "did" for himself or if he'd hired a part-time maid. He was perfectly capable of fending for himself. She'd discovered *that* about him when they'd lived together, and he had no hangups about pushing a vacuum cleaner around or wielding a sponge mop.

Breck had had enough. "Andrea, stop that!" he exploded.

Her head jerked up in shock. Breck's eyes were spitting blue fire and he looked dangerous. He faced

171

her, legs spread and hands on his hips, head slightly jutted forward in an attitude of belligerent exasperation.

"You've been gone six months without a word, then you suddenly appear, and all you do is make faces over my housekeeping. Good God, woman, I've been going slowly insane over these past months and you come in as cool as . . . as a damned cucumber! I want to know exactly where you've been and who you've been with and . . . oh, God, Andrea . . . you've got to let me kiss you!"

He surged across the space that separated them before she could react to his words and plucked her empty cup out of her hands with one hand. With the other hand he grasped her waist and pulled her toward him, sending her off-balance so that she lurched against his chest. He tossed the cup to the carpet, where it cracked but did not shatter, and used the hand thus unencumbered to finish pulling her up against the length of his body.

Andrea's mouth opened to protest hotly and that was all Breck needed. He kissed her with a reckless thoroughness that knocked the breath from her body and the stiffening from her knees. The unexpectedness of his assault on her senses pulled an initial response from her and for a long moment she reacted mindlessly to the starving ferocity of his kisses.

Her involuntary, instinctive response affected him strongly. He groaned and pulled her tightly to his intensely aroused body, his arms steel bands at her waist and shoulders. The tightness of his hold broke the momentary sensual delirium that was bidding fair to swamp Andrea's reason.

She began to fight him with a determined vigor, pushing at his shoulders and wrenching her mouth from beneath his. "Let me go, Breck!" she gasped, shoving fruitlessly against the encompassing strength of his powerful arms and shoulders. "Let . . . go . . . of . . . me!"

His arms slackened their crushing hold slightly, and she jerked away from him, panting and dishevelled. She pushed the hair back out of her eyes and glared murderously at him.

"Ahhh, that was nice." He grinned, unabashed and unrepentant. "It was nice even after you stopped cooperating," he said, bending down to rub his shin where she had kicked him as she struggled. His next words were slightly muffled by his stooped position, but she heard them clearly enough. "And while you did cooperate, it was heaven."

She couldn't retort that there had been precious little cooperation on her part, because it was so patently untrue. When their lips had met, even with such bruising force and ferocity, a torrent of passion had passed between them. It was sensual magic at its most potent, and she could not deny its existence between them. But she was no impressionable young virgin now, to be swept into a maelstrom of mindless surrender, so she was able to smile coolly at him and acknowledge his thrust.

"But you'll notice I quickly stopped cooperating, Breck, and the next time you try to leap on me like that, I won't cooperate at all from the very beginning. We'd better get something clear right now, Breck. I said it before, but it obviously bears repeating. I'm not your mistress anymore. Jeanne is dead and nothing will ever force me into such a situation again. I'm dependent on no one, answerable to no one, and that's the way it's going to stay. I'll be no man's mistress, especially yours!"

"Oh, yes you will, Andrea," Breck assured her in a goaded voice. "But there's something else you're going to be first . . . my wife."

CHAPTER SEVEN

Andrea, her mouth opening to hotly refute his arrogant assurances that he would succeed in making her his mistress once more, snapped it shut suddenly. She looked at him uncertainly, unwilling or unable to believe she had heard him correctly.

Breck rumpled his shining helmet of hair and pulled at the tie knotted at his throat, seeming to realize for the first time he was still in his suit. He hadn't even shed his coat, so preoccupied by Andrea's return that everything else had been forgotten.

"Blast it, Andrea, I hadn't planned to yell it out at you that way!" He took off his coat and vest and tossed them on the dining table, followed by his tie, which promptly slithered to the floor. He ignored it. He undid the first three buttons of his shirt and rolled back his shirtsleeves to mid-forearm.

"You make me lose control. You always have." He grinned a trifle sheepishly. "I guess you always will. Whenever I'm around you I react with my emotions instead of my brains—you turn those to mush —and see where *that's* gotten me." This time his smile was bitterly rueful.

Andrea bent to pick up the cup he had tossed on the carpet, and when she straightened back up, her face was guarded and watchful. She hadn't said a word since he had flung that pronouncement out between them like a gauntlet thrown down in a challenge to mortal combat. When she did speak, her voice matched his own for rueful overtones. "Just where has it gotten you, Breck?"

"It's gotten me into the position I'm in now, where the only woman I've ever loved and wanted to marry probably hates my guts," was his simple reply. "I want to marry you, Andrea. I want you for my wife, not my mistress."

"Why? Because you have no other hold on me, no way to force me to your will, so you offer marriage as a last resort?" Her voice was cutting.

"No! I've always wanted to marry you, from that very first night at the dance. I was jealous of McKay, afraid he was someone special to you. I wanted to take you home myself that night and I was only very slightly reassured when you said he was just your date."

He rubbed the back of his neck, trying to order his words coherently. "I would have asked you out the following night, but I was committed to go to New York for two weeks. The best I could do was maneuver you into going to Devon's opening night and go on from there."

They were still standing, facing each other like two antagonists getting ready to square off. Breck looked around a little helplessly, then gestured toward the couch. "Look, honey. I can see this is going to take some time. Sit on the couch and I'll get you a glass of wine and me a drink. I promise not to pounce again." He smiled slightly, but his eyes were sad and a little anxious.

"All right, Breck," Andrea agreed with surprising mildness, and some of the hair-trigger tension eased out of Breck's big body. She handed him the cup she still held and he carried it and his own cupful of cooled coffee back into the kitchen.

Andrea kicked off her shoes and curled up in a corner of the couch, awaiting his reappearance. She heard the clink of glassware and the opening and closing of the refrigerator and freezer doors. Soon Breck came back out, carrying the two glasses carefully. He handed her the nearly brimming glass and she took a sip. Liebfraumilch. She had seen the unopened bottle in the refrigerator when she had investigated earlier, rummaging for a snack. Put there by Breck as a sort of hostage toward her hoped-for return?

Breck sat down at the far end of the couch from her, cradling his glass down between his big hands, dwarfing it. He looked moodily into its amber depths and was silent for a while. Andrea merely watched him, prepared to wait until he was ready to speak.

He began abruptly. "Well, you went out with me, all right. Twice. And after that you weren't going to have anything to do with me. You meant it. I could tell."

The words were jerky, each one a piece of him ripped out by a barbed hook. "I was panicked . . . frantic . . . and so I behaved just about as badly as I could. I tried to make you respond to me sexually, to make you admit that you felt this magic as strongly as I did." He leaned forward and put his forearms and elbows on his knees, staring at the floor between his feet.

"I didn't know about all of your family history, but that was no excuse. When you just lay in my arms, so white and exhausted, I hated myself. You couldn't have despised me more just then than I did.

177

So I left. It was all I could do. Then I committed the greatest folly of all."

He got up and began to pace up and down. He tossed off the rest of his drink and set the empty glass atop the desk. "I tried to force you into marriage, and it blew up in my face. Andrea, you *have* to believe me. I wanted to marry you, not make you my mistress, and I would never have gone through with my threat to have your father arrested and Jeanne informed of his crimes. It was all bluff, and you called it.

"I thought that if I could get you to marry me, it would give you a chance to get to know me, to let me prove to you that I wasn't the sort of man your father is." His grating laugh hurt her to hear it. "Instead I turned out to be worse than he is, because I love you more than my life and all I did was hurt you, hurt you so badly that you ran away rather than let me comfort you when you needed it most.

"I don't know how to describe how I felt when you agreed . . . not to marry me as I had schemed . . . but to be my *mistress,* and for an extra fillip added that you'd never consider marriage with a man like me."

He sat back down on the couch and looked directly at her, the first time he had done so since he had started his explanation. "I was trapped. By now you hated me so much that if I had let the thing drop, you'd never have spoken to me again. You would never have believed I loved you and really wanted to marry you, and even if you had credited it, you'd only have laughed in my face."

There was stark agony on his face, and Andrea automatically stretched out a hand to him. "No! Let me finish it all. It has to be said, and done with." He continued, "So, I agreed, still hoping to get you to marry me. I was going to court you, if that's not too old-fashioned a term . . . take you out to dinner, dancing . . . and then you exploded another bombshell. I was to be allowed to visit you discreetly once or twice a week, like some cheap whore, and leave. I could have strangled you!" His expression was so ferocious, she believed him implicitly.

"I moved in with you. I was determined to make you get to know me, but I was also going to try my best not to force a sexual intimacy on you against your will. I hoped my forebearance would intrigue you, get you thinking about *why* I wasn't making love to you. It was sheer desperation, and when McKay called I let jealousy and my masculine territorial instincts goad me into making my claim on you very clear to him. It got rid of him, all right, but the price was too high. You found out, ripped into me, and—" His gesture said it all.

"All I could do then was hope your response to me was a sign that on some deep level you didn't hate me totally. If I could get you pregnant, or if, by living with me as my wife in daily intimacy, you could be brought to consider a marriage to me as something less than a fate worse than death . . . Oh, hell, Andrea . . ." he expostulated. "I had you. You slept so sweetly in my arms every night. . . . You were *mine,* and I was going to do everything in my power to keep you forever." He grinned at her, a tired twist of his mouth. "If I could have lived with you for seven years, at least you would have been my common-law wife."

His voice was draggingly husky, but he finished somberly. "When you left after Jeanne's death, I paid for every mistake. What if you *were* pregnant? You

179

were so vulnerable . . . what if you married someone on the rebound? I never knew I had such a fertile imagination. I'd run the gamut of every conceivable horrible possibility, and still wake sweating in the night with some new, devastating nightmare. You'd disappeared without a trace and believe me, I followed up every faint trail, even the most unlikely. I was resigned to waiting until you became a famous artist and tracking you down that way." He smiled, but his eyes were deadly serious.

"The only hope I had was this apartment. You kept the rent up . . . but even if you hadn't, I would have. In fact," he said rather sheepishly, "I've bought this building. As long as you kept up the rental, it was a link. So . . . I lived here and I waited."

"I meant it to be a link." She spoke so softly that he wasn't sure he had heard correctly. "I meant it as a message to you, Breck. Perhaps I didn't expect you to still be living here, but if . . . if you really cared about me, I knew you'd see the apartment as a sign that I'd come back to it someday. I didn't know how long it would take me or when I'd finish what I had to do, but I always planned to come back here."

Now it was Andrea's turn to search for words. She sipped meditatively at her wine, wine she had not touched during Breck's whole long recital. She decided the best thing was just to tell him baldly and hope he was able to understand.

"You know my family history, Breck, but I don't know if you can comprehend just what that situation did to me. I suppose I always knew that I didn't have a normally happy home life. Even though Jeanne loved my father, his endless affairs and betrayals still left their mark. How could they fail not to? They often fought, though not in front of me . . . but a child knows . . . and while Jeanne was all the mother a child could want or need, Devlin was a sometime father. He'd lavish attention in spurts and ignore me the rest of the time. I could never trust him as a child.

"As I grew older I began to understand the root of the tension between Jeanne and Devlin, and I also caught on that he was using me as a weapon against Jeanne. Those periods of attentive fatherhood always coincided with a crisis point between my mother and my father." Her lips twisted in a bitter grimace. "I was the ultimate blackmail weapon . . . knuckle under or he'd tell me the truth of my birth, was the message to Jeanne. Of course, I didn't understand until later just what threat he held over her, but I knew I was involved, was being used somehow to bring my mother to heel. From simply not trusting him I began to despise him. It made me very wary of all man-woman relationships and I never allowed myself to have a serious boyfriend."

Breck hadn't moved a muscle. He listened attentively to every word, concentrating as he had never concentrated before. What Andrea was telling him now would determine the course of their ultimate relationship. If Devlin Thomas had stood before him just at that moment, he might have killed him. Breck did not minimize his own culpability, but Devlin Thomas had a hell of a lot to answer for.

Andrea continued, sipping occasionally at her wine. "Then came Jeanne's accident and all the sordid revelations. I can't explain . . . there are no words . . . Oh, Breck, I felt so dirty and so guilty. Had Jeanne stayed with Devlin for my sake? What a heritage I had. . . . Would I someday come to be just like my father and my real mother? Added to the strain of Jeanne's condition and everything else, something snapped inside me. I began to hate Devlin, and that kind of hate is self-destructive. It twisted me inside and twisted my reactions to people . . . men in particular. Those three years of watching Jeanne's agony just made it worse."

She smiled slightly at him. "Then you came along. I was attracted to you, and you knew it. I'd never felt that way before and I fought it. When I was afraid I was losing that fight, I decided for my own peace of mind, I would never see you again. You see, I was sure you weren't thinking in terms of anything but an affair. To me you were a Viking, Breck. You'd take a woman as a warrior's recreation but leave without a backward glance. You were self-contained, self-sufficient, and I never thought of you in terms of marriage. Twisted perceptions . . ."

"Not so twisted, Andrea," Breck interjected softly. "That was the type of man I was before I met you. I'd never wanted commitments before."

She looked sadly at him. "I really hated you, Breck, when you threatened to hurt Jeanne. I didn't see it as bluff and I hated you, so I set out to hurt you in any way I could. I taunted you, used Johnny as a weapon, and precipitated the very situation I—we—both really wanted to avoid. I bear my guilts too, Breck."

She was feeling drained. These revelations were exhausting her and Breck noted with concern the pallor of her face and the tired droop of her shoulders.

"Andrea," he interrupted her, "when did you eat last? Let me heat you some soup or fix you a sandwich."

She smiled softly at him, and for the first time since she began to talk, Breck felt some coiled spring of tension relax slowly within him. She couldn't still hate him so much and smile at him like that.

"I had a snack while I was waiting for you to come back. I want to finish this, Breck, to clear away all the debris."

"At least let me get you some more wine." He leaned toward her and took the empty glass. Their fingers touched, and Breck's laid on hers for a momentary caress. She didn't jerk away, and he was again heartened.

When he came back with a less brimming glass than the first one, she continued her narrative. "You were right in a way, you know." He looked at her in comical astonishment, and she laughed slightly. "While I was living with you I certainly had to see you as a man, and get to know you. I couldn't escape you. You were everywhere. You were gentle with Jeanne, considerate of me, and even when we made love"—she met his eyes without blushing—"I couldn't stop responding to you. I knew that I had to get away, so I laid my plans, and when Jeanne died, I ran. I needed to be alone, and I knew you wouldn't consider our 'bargain' at an end with Jeanne's death. Even then I think I knew you weren't just after a short-term affair, but too much had happened to me. I needed time and to be absolutely away from all past associations. In earlier times ladies went to convents. I went to the sea. I had solitude and work and time to think. I had to decide just what I wanted from life and I had to get rid of the bitterness that was warping me. I had to let go of my hate for Devlin before it destroyed me as a person."

Her face reflected a little of the agony of mind she had experienced, and small muscles clenched along his jawline. "It took six months and it wasn't an easy process, but I cut out the hate. What Devlin did to Jeanne can't hurt me anymore. She's dead and at rest and he'll go to hell in his own way. I've let go at last, and I know what I want now."

"What do you want, Andrea? Tell *me* now." He seemed to brace himself to receive a mortal wound.

"I won't tell you, Breck. I'll show you."

She rose from the couch and held out one hand. He took her hand in his and she led him toward the studio. They entered and as she led him around to face the canvas on the easel, she said, "This is the last picture I painted before I came back. When it was done, I knew I was ready to come home."

Breck stood in front of the picture, spellbound. It was a scene of an ethereal fantasy. Two figures dominated the center of a fairy beach. A man, garbed in clothes suggestive of a long-ago Viking rover, carried a woman in his arms and was looking down at her. The woman was clad in an iridescent gown, which was molded lovingly around her figure. Something about the drape of the fabric against her legs and feet gave the impression of a mermaid's tail. It was not blatant, but the suggestion was unmistakable. He was obviously carrying her out of the sea, and small waves still crisped about his feet.

The woman lay trustingly in his cradling arms and in her hands she held a jeweled cup, intricately chased. She was offering it to him, and he was bending his head to drink, his eyes locked with hers. The man was Breck, the woman Andrea. The look was love.

"It's called *The Mermaid's Cup*, Breck." She spoke softly. "I think Gibran said it beautifully when he spoke of joy and sorrow. 'The deeper that sorrow carves into your being, the more joy you can con-

184

tain.' We've both been carved deeply by sorrow, my darling, but the cup has the capacity to hold full love at last. I am the mermaid, beloved. I offer you the cup of love, which never empties. Drink with me and of me and let us now share joy."

With an inarticulate sound of exultation Breck scooped her into his arms. As he carried his mermaid from the room his face was the face in Andrea's picture. The expression was love.

He carried her into the familiar bedroom, long uninhabited by both of them except in her saddest and sweetest dreams. He stopped by the side of the bed, swung her out of his arms, and slid her slowly down the waiting length of his body.

Andrea stood before him, head bent in an attitude of submission, as befits a captive, but she could hold the pose only for a moment. Breck tilted up her chin and searched her face with anxious eyes. What he saw, the love, the longing . . . all for him and for his touch . . . reassured him and he smiled.

With gentle, trembling hands he began to disrobe her, uncovering the only treasure that had reality and worth for him. His hands lingered over the globes of her breasts, cupping, caressing, delighting in the silky texture, which had no equal and no substitute. His thumbs traced and lightly flicked her nipples, which grew taut and aching beneath the expert stroke.

Andrea's eyes no longer watched him. Her eyelids had drifted shut, the better to savor the tactile pleasures of the flesh she had denied herself and him these long six months. She had not forgotten. She could never forget, but the pale fire of memory bore light resemblance to the consuming heat that now licked through the cells of her body.

185

Regretfully, but eagerly as well, his hands left the soft weight of her breasts and stroked downward to complete the task of undressing her. When she stood naked before him, his hungry eyes feasted on each curve and hollow and sweep of warm skin.

Her eyes opened languorously to watch him divest himself of his own hindering clothes, a task he completed much more efficiently than he had the removal of her own. A small, quiet smile tugged at her mouth. Breck saw it and leaned forward to kiss it onto his own mouth. It came to his lips but stayed with hers as well. A smile, like love, multiplies when shared.

They faced each other, delighting in the preliminary feast of eyes before they lay down to the banquet of taste and touch and scent. Andrea lifted her arms, offering. Breck stepped forward and lifted her once again, tilting her head back over the hard strength of his arm so that her throat and breasts arched up to his heated mouth. She moaned softly and her hand came up from her side to press his head more firmly against the rich curve he was so hungrily exploring.

He sank to the surface of the bed and, with unforgotten and desperate intensity, began to make her totally his once again.

Andrea gave herself, holding nothing, no shred of self back. Breck's mouth at her breasts, the drawing kisses and little, licking nibbles sent her nearly wild with sensation and desire. She ran her hands frenziedly over the corded muscles of his back, pulling him closer, urging him to take what she was so willing to admit was his.

They should be one. She had left him that she might come back to him at last, able to match him depth for depth. Now she was ready, eager, to both give and receive the full range of love. As Breck drew her beneath him, she arched up to meet him with an intensity that matched his own. They made love, they made life, they made a marriage.

LOOK FOR NEXT MONTH'S CANDLELIGHT ECSTASIES:

Dell Bestsellers